EMBERS OF HEALING

A Fated Mate, Damaged Hero, Forbidden Love, Orc Firefighter Romance

Aria Vale and Alana Khan

COPYRIGHT

Copyright © 2024 Alana Khan

All rights reserved.

No part of this publication may be reproduced, distributed, or transmitted in any form or by any means, including photocopying, recording, or other electronic or mechanical methods, without the prior written permission of the publisher, except as permitted by U.S. copyright law.

The story, all names, characters, and incidents portrayed in this production are fictitious and products of the author's imagination. No identification with actual persons (living or deceased), places, buildings, and products is intended or inferred and are entirely coincidental.

If you found this book outside of Amazon, it's likely a stolen/pirated copy. Authors make nothing when books are pirated. If authors are not paid for their work, they cannot afford to keep writing.

Criminal copyright infringement is investigated by the FBI and is punishable by up to 5 years in federal prison and a fine of $250,000.

For permissions contact: alanakhanauthor@gmail.com

St. Petersburg, FL 33709

www.alanakhan.com

COPYRIGHT   iii

Cover by AI Jenine Mante

CONTENTS

	Trigger warning	1
	Blurb	2
1.	Chapter One	4
2.	Chapter Two	10
3.	Chapter Three	13
4.	Chapter Four	17
5.	Chapter Five	21
6.	Chapter Six	24
7.	Chapter Seven	28
8.	Chapter Eight	33
9.	Chapter Nine	38
10.	Chapter Ten	42
11.	Chapter Eleven	44
12.	Chapter Twelve	47
13.	Chapter Thirteen	51
14.	Chapter Fourteen	55
15.	Chapter Fifteen	58
16.	Chapter Sixteen	63
17.	Chapter Seventeen	66

18.	Chapter Eighteen	70
19.	Chapter Nineteen	74
20.	Chapter Twenty	78
21.	Chapter Twenty-One	83
22.	Chapter Twenty-Two	87
23.	Chapter Twenty-Three	90
24.	Chapter Twenty-Four	95
25.	Chapter Twenty-Five	99
26.	Chapter Twenty-Six	102
27.	Chapter Twenty-Seven	112
28.	Chapter Twenty-Eight	118
29.	Chapter Twenty-Nine	121
30.	Chapter Thirty	126
31.	Chapter Thirty-One	131
32.	Chapter Thirty-Two	135
33.	Chapter Thirty-Three	140
34.	Chapter Thirty-Four	145
35.	Chapter Thirty-Five	151
36.	Chapter Thirty-Six	155
37.	Chapter Thirty-Seven	160
38.	Chapter Thirty-Eight	163
39.	Chapter Thirty-Nine	171
40.	Chapter Forty	175
41.	Chapter Forty-One	183
42.	Chapter Forty-Two: Epilogue	188
	Dear Reader	192

Sneak Peek: Ember's Spark	193
Many Thanks	207
About Alana Khan	208
Want more of my books?	209

TRIGGER WARNING

B rief reference to suicidal thinking.

BLURB

Injured in body and soul while protecting innocents from attack, the once-proud orc firefighter has withdrawn into bitter solitude. Will Sarah's desperate request for help be the key to unlock the damaged male hiding under his brooding green skin?

Sarah

The state's threat to condemn the house I inherited has left me racing against a looming deadline. In my desperation, I turn to an unlikely ally—the injured orc, Thornn, whose scars run as deep as his silence. I didn't have time to find anyone else to help, yet I doubt my decision the moment Thornn reluctantly agrees to provide muscle for the job.

I never imagined those bare, glistening muscles would be so enticing I'd yearn to lick them. Nor did I expect to discover the tender warrior spirit he hides under his wounded exterior.

Thornn

I'm broken. Ruined. To not inflict myself on my friends, I accept Sarah's job offer. I'm like a raw nerve—even her unfailing kindness pricks at me. I don't know whether to go for a long run to clear my head or pull her into my arms and kiss her senseless.

Except I can't keep my gaze off her as we work together, and I fist myself to sleep with images of her dancing in my mind.

Though I'm completely wrong for her, she's the perfect woman for me.

Want a copy of this book in audio for only $5.99? Go to shopalanakhan.com

CHAPTER ONE

Sarah

My hands are still fluttering with nerves as I approach the Integration Zone. I look at the letter on the driver's seat as though it's a mortal enemy. In a way, it is.

I opened the letter at my little condo less than an hour ago, freaked out so badly I couldn't think for long, panicked minutes, and then immediately called my best friend, Emma. She could tell I wasn't doing well and invited me to her apartment for comfort food and conversation. I don't remember making half the turns between my house and here. My hands seemed to be on autopilot as my mind spun with worry.

I return to my senses as I pull up to the gate at the entrance to the Zone. Though Emma has lived here with her orc mate, Kam, for months, I still get nervous at the military checkpoint that separates the Zone from the rest of Los Angeles.

Five thousand nagas, minotaurs, wolven, orcs, and other species previously known only in fairytales dropped to Earth over twenty-five years ago. Humans dubbed them "Others," and then rounded them up and shoved them into this fenced ghetto on the outskirts of the worst part of L.A. They've languished here since then.

The laws have loosened a bit over time. They're allowed out on work permits, but they can still be paid one-third of minimum wage, and they aren't allowed to live outside the gates. I've become familiar with the Others, but it's the gangs of Purist protesters who often swarm outside the gates that terrify me.

I state my business to the National Guard soldier at the gate and she waves me through. The Zone dwellers try their best to keep it clean, but the poverty here is stark, and it always seems I'm traveling back in time when I pass through the gates.

I take that back. It's not just back in time when I visit this ten-block area whose buildings were built in the 50s or earlier. But into another world with blue-scaled nagas, towering horned minotaurs, and shaggy, wary wolven.

I make my way to Emma and Kam's apartment, letter in hand, and am relieved to slide inside her place to the smells of her signature Taco Soup. Her gentle hug helps slow my racing heart.

"So, this is the letter that's made you lose your mind? Can I read it?" She thrusts her open palm at me, then slides onto the couch, motioning me to join her on the other end.

Yes. My head is spinning, and the world is tilting under my feet because of this official notice I just received about the property in Colorado I inherited from Aunt Beth three months ago.

Emma has been my best friend since college. We were inseparable, sharing dating disasters—well, *her* dating disasters, I didn't date much, then went with Liam my whole senior year—as well as navigating college and jobs. Then she met Kam, who loves her more than life itself. She moved to the Zone recently when they were married—they call it mated.

At first, I tried not to like him because loving an Other is dangerous, but he's just so good to her, and *for* her. The impulsive scatterbrain who was my friend has grown into herself since they've been together. That's why I'm here. I hope she can calm me down and help me decide what to do next.

"Shit. Why can't they write this so a layperson can understand it?" She shakes her head, sounding as exasperated as I felt trying to figure out all the legalese. Tucking a foot under her other thigh, she settles into the couch as she tries to parse through the letter.

She reads parts of it out loud, but I read it at every stoplight on my way here and can now almost recite it by heart. My palms sweat when she reads, "'An inspection has been conducted in response to an anonymous report regarding potential health and safety hazards.' Blah blah, 'the aforementioned property exhibits conditions indicative of hoarding, posing a risk to the safety and well-being...' Why don't they get to the point? 'You are hereby mandated to promptly undertake comprehensive cleaning and remediation efforts.'"

She glances at me and must notice how lost I look because she says, "Okay, I'm scanning now. 'Failure to complete the prescribed remediation within one month will result in legal proceedings, including but not limited to the condemnation and demolition of the property.'"

She scoots closer to me and uses her most soothing tone, "You have a whole month, Sarah. You can fix this. I mean, how bad can it be?"

Just as I'm about to elaborate on exactly how bad this can be, Kam walks in the door. He's the sweetest male, even if he has a terrible sense of humor.

"Knock knock! Who's there? Kam. Kam who? Kam to join the fun!"

Perhaps he notices the sweat beading above my upper lip, or the frown lines on my forehead, because he tries to break the mood.

"Why the long faces? This is a no-frowning zone."

Emma's scolding, "Kam!" settles him down as he slides into the chair opposite the couch and, in a serious tone, says, "Whatever's going on, I'll try to help."

I don't need another invitation to explain things as I vomit out all my worries. "It's a thousand and fourteen miles away, for one, in Verdant Park, Colorado. We had the funeral here since we're her only relatives."

CHAPTER ONE

I thought I was over the worst of my grief, but having to revisit these details makes me pause a moment to control the tears threatening to spill down my cheeks.

"Her lawyer completed the paperwork transferring ownership of the property to me. I should have visited, but you know how busy I've been with my dissertation."

After folding the letter, I absently slide my fingernail along the crease.

"I haven't visited Aunt Beth since I was ten. That was when she quit inviting me to Colorado and took me on cruises instead. Now that I know about the hoarding, I imagine that's why she didn't want me to visit her home. Which means she's been hoarding for over a decade. And the house is huge. I guess you could call it a mansion."

They both know my family is wealthy, but I always feel a little weird when the topic arises.

"Still, Sarah, no matter how big the house is, this is doable. You have a month," Emma is using her calmest voice.

For a split second, I'm lulled out of my anxiety, but then it returns with the power of a tsunami and I list all the reasons I'm freaking out. "I can't just hire a bunch of guys to help. Aunt Beth told me she had lots of money in bearer bonds and gems hidden all over the mansion, said she didn't trust banks."

This earns me wide eyes from them both. I imagine this sounds to them like less of a nightmare and more of a dream come true—bearer bonds, gems. Perhaps they're thinking of it like a treasure hunt—except they're not picturing all those valuables hidden under a thousand pounds of detritus.

"If I just hire a bunch of day laborers, they'll want to throw everything away before I have a chance to go through it. The idea of bonds or jewels being tossed into a dumpster breaks my heart. Those things were important to my aunt. They're a connection to her that I don't want severed. She always seemed so distracted and uncomfortable with all the money, but said more than once that she wanted me to do something good with it after she was gone."

They're true friends, not judging. Instead, they remain focused and drill down to gather all the facts. I can see why Emma loves this male enough to change her life and live in the Zone with him. Terrible jokes aside, he has the biggest heart and can be so supportive, not just to her, but to me.

When I first looked at him, all I could see were his gleaming ivory tusks, amber eyes, and green skin. Now what grabs my attention are his amazing good looks and what a great guy he is. Behind those jutting fangs, he's got the warmest, most genuine smile I've ever seen.

When I'm done laying out all the facts and my worries, my two friends gaze at each other, look back at me, and say in unison, "Thornn."

They explain that Thornn was the orc firefighter who left the safety of the Integration Zone to rescue them the night the Purist haters assaulted them. My two friends managed to make their way to safety. Thornn wasn't so lucky.

When he was finally dragged back into the Zone by his friends, he'd been beaten so badly he had several fractured bones, a knife slash across his abdomen, and a broken tusk. They'd even hacked off his braids.

I feel a pang of renewed fear for my friend, but more than anything, hatred at those bigots bubbles inside me.

"He hasn't been the same since," Kam says with a sad shake of his head. "He doesn't talk. Chief Brokka Googled it, says it's called selective mutism. All I know is, he's really fucked up. Brokka can't let him work as a firefighter anymore. When fighting fires, we have to communicate or someone could die. Without work, he's lost his housing. He's been couch surfing—"

Emma interrupts to add, "He stayed here for a week, then went to stay with another crew member, not wanting to wear out his welcome. He's been going from friend to friend for months.

CHAPTER ONE

Thornn's a perfect gentlemale, Sarah." By the soothing tone of her voice, it's clear she knows I'm hating this idea with a passion.

"He's a hard worker and would give you the shirt off his back," Kam adds, his normally happy face now a mask of pain.

I get it. Thornn was injured in a life-changing manner because he went into the streets during a riot to rescue Kam and Emma. Kam looks as though he has a healthy dose of survivor guilt.

I ask a few more questions and am quiet and thoughtful during dinner, not tasting a bite. I have a long, labored internal debate with myself. In the end, I realize I'd rather hire someone my friends know and trust than pick up a crew of day laborers when I arrive in Colorado.

When I give Kam the go-ahead to text Thornn a job offer at $20 an hour, he beams at me and winks. "Besides, you're guaranteed he won't talk your ear off."

I have a dissertation to write and a cozy condo here in L.A. The last thing I want is a cross-country drive with a mute orc. But I can't let them condemn and bulldoze the house I inherited. It's where I had so many fun visits with an aunt I loved.

I don't see another option, and the clock is ticking.

CHAPTER TWO

Thornn

My friend wants to offer you a job. $20 an hour. Interested?

Kam is a great guy with terrible jokes and a penchant for talking. His texts are usually longer than this.

If the lack of details didn't send up a red flag, the hourly wage sure does. In California, orcs can be paid $5.43 an hour. Who in their right mind would offer four times that amount?

I busy my mind with math because the real issue is much harder to focus on. I've been depending on my friends for months, ever since Chief Brokka had to let me go from the fire department because I'm so fucked up I can't work.

Well, that's not true. I can work. I just can't talk.

As much as I hate imposing on friends, there's a silver lining to being obligated to socialize. If I was still living alone in my apartment, I might have given in to my frequent impulse to off myself. There have been a few times when the only thing keeping me alive was my desire not to traumatize my friends when they woke up to find my cold body on their couch.

I'm better now. Even if I wasn't, it's time to quit depending on my friends for housing.

At twenty bucks an hour, it wouldn't take too long to save up first and last month's rent. The Zone is a pit and we're treated like shit, but at least the Integration Zone Housing Authority has kept our rent low enough that most of us can keep a roof over our heads.

What's the catch? I ask.

Of course, there has to be a catch. No one in their right mind would pay an Other so much money.

Emma's friend Sarah needs muscle. I told her you've got plenty of it.

Sounds like a one-day job. Not to look a gift horse in the mouth, but that won't get me enough to move out on my own.

Needs help moving? I wonder why he doesn't just tell me all the details.

Kind of. She needs help cleaning out her aunt's house. Says it's like an episode of Hoarders.

Good. That will take at least a couple of days.

She knows I don't talk?

Yeah. No problem.

Before I can respond, I see the three dots rolling... for a while. Either he's writing a book, or he's writing and erasing. Either way, I think I'm about to find out the catch because there's got to be a reason she's willing to pay so much.

The job's in Colorado. She'll drive you there and back. Give you room and board. I met her the same time I met Emma, so I've known her a while. She's a good person.

When I don't respond immediately, he adds, *It will do you good.*

Even though he's doing me a favor, I can't control the quick flare of anger that thrums through my veins. How dare he pretend to know what will do me good?

I picture the trip to Colorado smashed in a car with a human I don't know and imagine being out of the Zone for who knows how long. Humans hate Others. Not just the Purists, though they're the most vocal. Many humans look at us with fear, if not hatred.

And then there's what happened on the night that changed my life forever. My tusk wasn't the only thing they broke that night. Fuckers.

I'm built big. Muscled. Yet the idea of leaving the Zone, entering the human world, makes my belly clench in fear.

Do you want to meet her? She's at our place right now.

No.

I responded so fast, I'm not sure if my "no" was in response to meeting her or was "no" to the job.

Before I can overthink it, I type, *I don't need to meet her. I'll take the job.*

I may not want it, but I need it.

Five minutes later, we've hammered out all the details. She'll pick me up at the front gate at 6:00 a.m. the day after tomorrow. Kam told me to pack for a couple of weeks. That put my guts in a twist. Two weeks outside the Zone, working in close quarters with a human.

Shit. What have I gotten myself into?

CHAPTER THREE

Sarah

How can I be bone tired at 5:50 a.m.? It's going to be a long day and I've barely started.

I spent most of yesterday on the phone taking care of business. First, I texted my parents, who left on a cruise the day before I received the letter from the Colorado authorities. They'll be gone for weeks on what's called a repositioning cruise as they cross the ocean with only a few stops. My text was businesslike, not even hinting at how overwhelming this felt. I didn't want them to worry about me.

When they didn't text back immediately, I rolled my eyes. They have enough money for a cruise, but for some reason, they balk at the high price of Wi-Fi on the ship. They're out in the middle of the ocean with very few stops and might not get my text for days. That's probably a good thing. I imagine they wouldn't be happy if they knew I was going to be in close quarters with an orc for the next few weeks.

The rest of the day, I dealt with things in Colorado, including ordering a large roll-off trash container for the front yard. Although I haven't seen my aunt's house since she started hoarding, I imagine that by the time all is said and done, that will be the first of many roll-offs that will be hauled to the dump.

I made sure the water and lights were on; wouldn't want to have to deal with that once we're there. I don't think an orc will be welcome in any motel or hotel in America while we wait for the house to be habitable.

People in L.A., especially near the Zone, are at least aware of Others. Sometimes they can be spotted in public doing hot, labor-intensive jobs like road construction. As much prejudice as there is against them, the lure of hiring competent help at one-third minimum wage is hard to resist.

But out in the hinterlands of Utah and Colorado, Thornn is going to terrify people. And terrified people often want to attack what they don't understand. So I need to get us all the way to the Colorado mountains in one day with as few pit stops as possible.

He says he knows how to drive. I'm just not sure I trust him to drive my Subaru Forester, even though he's licensed to drive the fire engine. At some point, though, I imagine I'll need a nap.

As I wait to be allowed through the Zone gate, I see Kam on the other side of the gate with another orc at his side. It's hard to tell what the male looks like, other than that those wide shoulders look as though they'll come in handy moving heavy trash when we get to my aunt's. Well, I guess it's not my aunt's house anymore. It's mine.

He's in an army-green hoodie, the hood pulled low enough to cover part of his face. There's a black duffle at his feet, stuffed to the gills.

I pull over just inside the gate. Until recently, Others weren't allowed out of the Zone except to go to their jobs. Few have disposable income, so there are few cars in the Zone—no traffic. It's no problem for me to park by the curb for introductions—which are awkward.

Thornn's fists are jammed into the sweatshirt's pockets, so I don't attempt to shake his hand. I give him a perky, "Hello," which he responds to with a curt, barely there nod. Two minutes later, his duffle is stowed in the back, along with all my suitcases, and we're off.

CHAPTER THREE 15

"I've got water and snacks behind the front seat. Figured we'd want them later. Want me to stop for coffee? Food?" I ask as we traverse the city streets before we hit the highway.

It takes a moment of silence before I realize I need to look at him to catch his response. When I glance at him, he shakes his head, so I keep driving.

I put on a Spotify playlist I made for the trip, then tell him, "If my taste in music makes you crazy, just let me know. I'm sure we can find something we both like."

Once we're on the highway, I say, "Google says it's about fifteen hours. I figure with stops for food and gas, we'll be lucky to make it by midnight. Just let me know if you're hungry, thirsty, or have to pee."

Though I hadn't noticed him carrying it, he lifts a brown paper bag from the floor. After pulling out a bottled water, which he sets in his cupholder, he shows me a sandwich, which he then shoves back into the bag. I control my scoff. He's a mountain of a male. How's he going to survive all day on one sandwich and a bottle of water?

It's not just his wide shoulders, he's big everywhere. It makes the interior of my roomy SUV feel as though I'm driving a toy. His hood brushes the roof, and the top of his shoulder is above my eye level. With him being silent, I might as well be sitting next to a stone gargoyle.

"Even though we have water and snacks in the car, I'll need a few pit stops along the way."

I catch a nod out of the corner of my eye before he turns to look out his window, leaving me a view of the back of his hoodie.

I didn't really catch a good look at him in the early morning gloom. When will I be able to see his face, I wonder.

Kam made sure to tell me about Thornn's broken tusk. "Our tusks are like our crowning glory. They signify a female's beauty." He paused, gave Emma a molten gaze, then added, "Except for you, love. You're so beautiful you have no need for tusks."

After she blew him a kiss, he continued. "Our tusks, our long braids, and our tats are outward signs of a male's masculinity. I imagine the shorn hair and broken tusk make him feel like less of a male."

Perhaps that's why it's lunchtime and I've yet to catch a glimpse of Thornn's face.

"It looks like there's a bunch of fast-food places at the next exit. I'm starved. There's a Mickey D's, Hardees, Taco Bell. Have any preference?"

All I get is another headshake. It's already been a long, quiet day, and we still have eight hundred miles to go.

"Need to pee?" I ask and am not surprised when he shakes his head. "What am I getting you?" Headshake.

As I open my door, planning on getting him a couple of sandwiches and some fries even if he says he doesn't want anything, he reaches out and grips my wrist so softly it takes me a moment to realize he's touching me.

He immediately snatches his hand back, reaches for his phone, and starts texting.

Please don't park here. Everyone can see me. Can you pull around back?

Although he's still facing away from me so I can't see his face, I can almost hear the pleading tone in his text. Seeing this big, strong male be so afraid of humans makes my stomach knot.

"Sure. No worries." I pull to the back of the lot and park with his door so close to the dumpster no one could walk on his side of the car. "How's this?"

Head nod.

As I walk to the restaurant door, I try to picture what awaits me at the mansion so I can calculate how long it will take to clean the house, pass an inspection, and return to my regular life. This might just turn out to be the longest couple of weeks of my life.

CHAPTER FOUR

Thornn

My stomach is in knots, has been since before she pulled into the Zone this morning. I've been riding the waves of panic since we left the gates.

I have no health insurance. Even if I did, there aren't any therapists who work with Others. Being honest with myself, I admit I probably wouldn't see one even if I had access. A few months ago, I couldn't have imagined contemplating asking for psychological help.

But the Internet is free, and I've been reading and watching videos on how to deal with what I've diagnosed as my PTSD. So, for the past several hours, I've been looking at the passing scenery and counting my breaths. Maybe it's helping. Otherwise, I think I'd be having a full-on panic attack, complete with hyperventilation and the sweats.

With her out of the car, I take a moment and slow my racing heart. It's better with her gone. My heart is almost back to normal when she returns and hands me a bag.

"I didn't know what you'd want, so I got you a Big Mac and a quarter pounder, plus some fries."

With that, she pulls out and we're on the road again. I'm sure she thought she was doing me a favor by buying the food, but the smell is making my stomach roll.

"You know, my car will read your text messages out loud to me. I thought maybe we could talk."

No. I didn't know a car could read texts, not that I want to talk. It's everything I can do to keep my shit together. Then I realize how uncomfortable my silence must be. And how rude. The poor woman is doing me a favor, giving me a job, paying me a lot of money, and has been nothing but kind. I should talk to her.

Test, I type.

A moment later, a chime comes through the dash and a robotic female voice says, "Test." It's going to be odd hearing my words come out as a woman's voice, but it will allow me to talk to Sarah during our long trip.

"Cool, huh? I'm not a fan of long-distance driving. Talking will make the time go faster."

I have no idea what to talk about, but one thing I know is that if I don't say something soon, she's going to start asking me questions, which is the last thing I want.

Tell me about this house and why you own it when you live in L.A.

"My Aunt Beth had no children, and I was the only niece or nephew. She died earlier this year and left her house to me. Visiting it and deciding what to do with it was on my list of things to do after I finished writing my dissertation. I figured the house could wait until I had time to come deal with it. I hadn't visited in over a decade and was shocked when I got the letter saying it had been reported as a safety hazard. When they investigated, they found she had so much stuff hoarded inside that if I don't clean it out, they're going to condemn the place."

Sounds like a disaster, but I imagine it won't take long to clear out the shack and get back to the Zone.

Sorry to hear that.

"Yeah. It's a shame. I always loved the mansion. It was built by a guy who made a fortune in the Colorado Silver Boom of the

CHAPTER FOUR 19

late 1800s. Aunt Beth married into the family. The property is beautiful, too. You won't have to worry about neighbors. It's on a huge parcel of land."

Mansion? Silver boom? Does Sarah realize she's talking to a male who was born in the Integration Zone and has lived in state-sponsored housing his whole life?

I'm sorry you lost your aunt. Sounds like you were close. Don't worry, I'll help you clean it out. I'm handy and might be able to fix things up if you need.

Handy by necessity. Living in the Zone, we had to learn how to fix what we had since there wasn't money to buy new.

"Thanks. That's kind of you. My only goal is to clean it and pass inspection so they don't condemn it."

With the silence broken, we actually carry on a conversation off and on for the next several hours. She's led an interesting life, traveled a lot, and is working on her doctoral dissertation. Said she couldn't decide between English and Psychology, so she combined them.

"Don't laugh when you hear the title of my dissertation." She warns me. "It's 'The Role of Sleep in Shakespearean Tragedies: A Psychoanalytic Approach'."

Are you speaking English?

She laughs, "I get it, but that's academia for you. I'm analyzing the use of sleep in Shakespeare's tragedies and exploring its psychological implications for the characters."

Sounds like your dissertation might be good for putting readers to sleep.

The moment I push send, I realize that when the robotic voice reads it, it might not come out as I intended it. For the first time today, I push my hood off and try to put a smile on my face so she can see I was joking.

"I get it. You're not the first person to kindly tell me it doesn't sound like a bestseller. But if it succeeds in getting me my doctorate, I'll be happy."

She glances over, a teasing smile lighting up her face. I've been so busy avoiding her, it's the first time I've gotten more than a glimpse of her. She's pretty.

Her brown hair shines in the afternoon sunlight, framing delicate features and wide sapphire eyes that sparkle with humor and intelligence. Her skin is flawless, her upturned nose dusted with freckles. She's not skinny, like so many human women on TV. It looks as though she's sturdy and won't be shy about helping me muck out her house... mansion.

Something in her smile makes me glad I dredged up the nerve to look at her. For some reason, I want to make her laugh again just to see the way it lights up her face. She seems open and approachable, drawing me in with her quirky mind and thirst for knowledge.

I dare a longer glance at her slender neck and the elegant line of her jaw. She wears no makeup that I can see, so I can appreciate her natural beauty. She smells good too, but for the life of me, I can't name the base notes or accents in her scent. There's something green in it, maybe fresh-cut ivy and something earthy like olive oil. But that is how far above me she is. Her fragrance is alien to the likes of me.

Maybe it's the long drive wearing me down, but in this unguarded instant, I feel an unexpected clench in my chest that has nothing to do with anxiety. I quickly look away before she catches me staring.

CHAPTER FIVE

S arah

Emma and I need to have a serious talk the first time I have a free moment. She said Thornn spent a week on her couch. She knows him. She couldn't have mentioned that he's movie-star handsome? Well, that is, if orcs could be movie stars.

He's freaking gorgeous. Kam said an orc's tusks were his crowning glory? Well, Thornn's freaking *face* is his crowning glory. The broken tusk? Who could even notice it when he looks like *that*?

I decide to memorize this moment with the afternoon light catching his ruggedly handsome features. He has sharp cheekbones and a strong jawline that speak of his orc heritage, yet he possesses an elegant bone structure that's oddly beautiful.

His skin is a rich jade that makes his amber eyes glow like embers. He watches me carefully through thick dark lashes. His almost-black hair hangs to his shoulders in waves. The fact that he's the only orc with hair that doesn't fall almost to his waist must be hard for him, but, in my opinion, it highlights his sharp cheekbones, broad forehead, and strong jaw.

I clutch the steering wheel more tightly because I have the strangest urge to run my hands through it. His pointed ear, what you'd see on an elf in a movie, looks perfect peeking out between those dark strands. I briefly imagine a scantily clad Henry Cavill emerging from a fantasy forest, dyed green with pointy ears, and decide that even *he* couldn't hold a candle to Thornn.

As he gives me a hint of a smile, it highlights the jagged remains of his right tusk and the shadows of pain in his eyes. But the imperfect tusk does nothing to diminish his allure. If anything, it adds to his roguish charm.

Even though I've seen Kam's black tongue a hundred times, it startles me when Thornn's slips between his lips. I'll never understand in a million years why such a thing strikes me as shockingly sexy. Maybe because it highlights his Otherness.

He's broad-shouldered and muscular, his formidable size evident even sitting down. I sense coiled power and quick reflexes beneath that calm exterior.

When he catches me staring, I swiftly turn my gaze back to the road, cheeks warming. I steel my nerves and risk another side-eye glance. One thing is certain, with his mix of strength and vulnerability, Thornn is dangerously appealing. The next few weeks just got a whole lot more complicated.

"I shouldn't have gotten the large soda," I say as I turn into a highway rest station in the middle of nowhere, Utah. I pull right in front, assuming the male has got to go by now. Even if he was made of steel, he can't hold it forever. "I pulled up close so you could get in and get out as quickly as possible."

He texts me, but since the car is turned off, the female voice doesn't read it out loud. He turns the screen to me.

No. Please.

I start the car and pull around the rear of the large rest station which backs up to a treed area.

"This okay?"

He nods, but his hoodie is back up and he's slouching to avoid notice, as if that position will hide the fact that he's built like a linebacker.

CHAPTER FIVE

I hurry to the cinderblock bathroom, do my business, and return to the car in record time.

"Okay, Thornn. I've got an idea."

I open the rear door on the passenger side and say, "Just ease out of the car. With both doors open, and me standing between them with my back to you, you'll be boxed in on all four sides. Do your business and we'll be on our way. No muss, no fuss."

He turns to look at me, an unfathomable expression hiding behind his wide, amber eyes. I imagine if he didn't have to go so badly, we'd have a little argument via text. Instead, he eases out of the car and waits for me to get into position. The moment my back is turned to him, I hear the metallic clicking of his zipper, then the soft patter of his urine on the leaf-strewn blacktop.

This is a proud male enduring a shitty time in his life. Having to urinate in public may not faze him at all, but doing it six inches from a human woman he just met couldn't be the highlight of his week.

To cover the sound of his humiliation, I sing the words to "Don't Worry, Be Happy" including the ooh, ooh, oohs.

The moment he's finished, we pile back into the car and are on our way.

The song? He asks.

"'Don't Worry, Be Happy'? Bobby McFerrin? I thought everyone on the planet was familiar with that one. It's quite the earworm."

Why? Why the song?

Because he asked, I imagine he knows, but I tell him anyway. "I thought it might make the moment less... embarrassing for you."

Thank you.

CHAPTER SIX

T hornn

Although I offered to drive several times throughout the trip, Sarah finally took me up on it about six hours ago. When she took a nap, I could finally relax and not worry about having to communicate. It was as though I breathed easily for the first time today.

I snuck glances at her sleeping form from time to time. She's a pretty woman, but I think what I like best about her is how nice she is. I still feel awkward around her, but she's tried hard to put me at ease. 'Don't Worry, Be Happy'—that was odd, but nice of her.

We switched places when we got to Denver, and since then we've been climbing steadily uphill toward her house... well, it sounds as though I should call it a mansion.

The headlights cut through the inky night as we make the final turn up the long, winding driveway. As we crest the top of the hill, I can just make out the imposing silhouette of the house, backlit by the starry sky. There couldn't be more stars in the sky than there were in L.A. Could there? I guess it's that we're out in the middle of nowhere.

As we draw nearer, the fine details come into focus in the headlights. My breath catches at the sight—I've never seen anything so grand and ornate in my life. Lately, we've been allowed to go on fire calls outside the Zone, but there's nothing like this in the parts of L.A. I've traveled. It's obvious why Sarah

CHAPTER SIX 25

called this a mansion. I've watched enough renovation shows on TV to know what I'm looking at.

Built of weathered red brick and carved sandstone, turrets and gables jut from the steeply pitched slate roof. Intricate stonework and wrought-iron railings adorn the wraparound porch and balconies. The windows glint in the moonlight, hinting at the fortunes that must have been spent to construct this place in the late 1800s, the heyday of the Colorado silver boom. I can almost hear the fancy parties and picture the socialites who once must have visited here.

We pull up the circular drive, tires crunching on the gravel, and the engine's rumble fades to silence. As I step from the car, the crisp mountain air fills my lungs. Although this part of the world is new to me, my enhanced orc nose identifies pine, snow, and woodsmoke. Somewhere an owl hoots. This is my first taste of a season other than the eternal summer of Southern California.

Rubbing my arms against the chill, I follow several paces behind Sarah as she approaches the five steps leading to imposing carved oak doors. The mix of emotions she must be going through is unimaginable, as she returns to a place that holds countless memories of her aunt who passed away. Does she regret not coming back sooner? Does she fear entering the house, not knowing what state of chaos awaits inside after years of her aunt's hoarding?

My heart clenches for her as she fumbles to fit the key in the lock and pushes hard against the swollen door to force it open. An avalanche of junk mail and newspapers cascades over the threshold to scatter at our feet. Sarah gazes upward into the dark foyer and lets out a trembling sigh. "Home sweet home."

As Sarah eases into the house, the stench hits me like a sledgehammer. I double over, gagging as the fetid air violates my sensitive nose. The reek is an unholy mixture of decaying food, excrement, piss, and mold that turns my stomach.

It's a testament to the solid construction of the house and well-sealed windows that I couldn't smell it until the door opened.

Bile surges up my throat. I slap a hand over my mouth, but it's useless against the hellish, stinking stew. My eyes warm with unshed tears as I stumble back through the doorway onto the porch, then grip the railing as I hang my head over the side and puke violently into the rose bushes below.

My insides cramp with the force of my retching. The sound and smell make it worse, but I can't stop. An orc's nose is ten times more sensitive than a human's. This reek is sheer torture, violating me right down to my cells.

I hear Sarah escape outside, gagging. The stench clings to me, in my hair, my clothes. I straighten, swaying with nausea and lightheadedness. Misery and revulsion roil through me.

Sarah's disgusted face probably mirrors mine. My heart plummets. We haven't yet begun and already this task seems impossible.

Even as I consider calling my friends from the department and begging them to come retrieve me—in a fire engine if necessary—Sarah sprints off the porch, yanks open the Forrester's back door, and comes running back to me, two bottles of water in each hand.

"Here!"

She's panting as she lays three bottles on the wooden porch step, cracks a bottle, and hands it to me when I join her at the bottom of the steps. As I gulp the entire bottle down, I watch her drink and spit and drink some more. In between swings, she makes disgusted sounds.

She pauses a moment to say, "This must be terrible for you. Kam told me orcs have a heightened sense of smell."

I drink my second bottle more slowly, trying Sarah's swish-and-spit technique, though it seems no more effective than downing the bottle in one long guzzle. She gave me a drink before she took her own because she knew it affected me more than her. I've never known a human to put me first before. This baffles me.

CHAPTER SIX 27

Holding my breath as I turn toward the house, I take the porch steps two at a time and close the door to stop the fetid stench from seeping out, then dig deep inside my soul as I approach her. When I have her full attention, I find the strength from somewhere inside me to find the voice I thought I'd lost forever to croak, "Thanks."

CHAPTER SEVEN

Sarah

From what Emma and Kam told me, that's the first word Thornn has uttered in months. I don't want to make a big deal out of it, but it's a pretty important landmark. I decide to lance him with a piercing gaze and simply say, "You're welcome," as we walk toward the car.

"We can't sleep inside." I'm thinking out loud. "And I doubt you'd agree to a motel."

His adamant head shake was hardly necessary. After his near meltdown at McDonald's, it's clear he couldn't tolerate that kind of scrutiny from humans in a public place. To be honest, I'm not sure he'd be safe.

"So here's what I propose. Aunt Beth used to have some furniture on her rear deck." I recall some pretty comfy outdoor lounge chairs, but that was over a decade ago. "Let's go around back and scout it out. If there's only one chair, I'll sleep in the car. It's nippy. Let's bring some clothes and layer up. Who knows?" I shrug, sounding far more perky than I feel. "Maybe things will look better in the morning."

He good-naturedly rolls his eyes. We both know that even if things *look* better in the morning, they certainly aren't going to *smell* better.

CHAPTER SEVEN   29

We round the back of the house and I see through the spacious, covered, screened porch that the lounge chairs have been replaced by one big round outdoor bed.

"Way to go, Aunt Beth." I'm sure my sarcasm is obvious.

I know why she bought this thing. On one of our cruises, we spent a lot of time on a bed just like this when we hung out at the pool. The base is wicker, and the mattress is covered in sturdy beige canvas. It's about six feet in diameter, which was great when Aunt Beth and I shared it. Not so much for an orc who must be well over six feet tall with shoulders almost a yard wide.

I climb the steps to the porch, looking around in the dim moonlight to see if maybe one of the old loungers is folded and leaning against a wall. No such luck. With all the shit she collected, why would she get rid of the lounge chairs? At least the porch isn't full of clutter.

In fact the space is surprisingly clean. I turn to open the plexiglass sliders that cover the screens to find Thornn opening the last one.

Thornn reaches into his pocket and texts me: *I'll be fine in the car if I lay the seat back. You take this bed.*

"The stench is stuck in my nose, but I don't smell anything from the porch. Can you Thornn?"

He pauses and hesitatingly inhales a little bit more than the shallow breaths we've both been making. He gives me a small, relieved smile and a headshake.

For the next several minutes, we have a very interesting half-text/half-spoken argument. I won't hear of the poor guy folding himself like an origami project to sleep in my car. He, on the other hand, is adamant that it's no place for me, either. When I overrule his suggestion that he sleep on the porch floor, we both realize there's only one choice left.

"Okay. We'll share the bed. I'm sure you'll be a perfect gentlemale." That wasn't sarcastic. After spending the day with him, I trust him not to make an inappropriate move.

And I'm sure you'll be a perfect gentlewoman and my virtue will remain intact. His unexpected humor startles a laugh out of me.

I can feel the breeze coming through the screen, blowing toward the front of the house.

I rummage in the dark and find a t-shirt in the bag I carried from the car, then tie it around my face in a terrible impression of an Old West bank robber. When he tilts his head in question, I say, "If I'm not back in five minutes, send a posse."

Before he can argue, or maybe he's texting me as fast as his fingers can fly and just hasn't pushed send yet, I try the back door and am not surprised to find it unlocked. After grabbing one last breath of fresh air, I hurry inside and turn on a light.

It's worse than my worst imaginings. I don't waste any time thinking about it. Using the open paths, I jog from room to room to open every window on the front and sides of the house. Thankfully, at least one window in every room on the ground floor was unobstructed. If I open rear-facing windows, I'm sure the odor will be too rank for us to tolerate.

Hopefully the wind will continue to blow toward the front of the house.

My mission is accomplished at lightning speed, and I emerge onto the back porch to see the handsome orc, his lips pursed in a disapproving scold as he points to his phone.

I'm not surprised when I read his irritated, *What the fuck!?! Squatters could have been lying in wait for you. You should have let me do that.*

I've spent close to twenty-four hours in close proximity to him. In that time, he's been sad, terrified, and angry. This latest text, though, seems to reveal more of the true Thornn than anything he's said or done up to this point. I like that he finally feels comfortable enough with me to show his genuine self.

CHAPTER SEVEN 31

"Wow! Three punctuation marks. You've outdone yourself. First of all, squatters would rather die of exposure than stay a minute inside that house. Second, you wouldn't get ten feet inside without barfing."

He shakes his head in disgust, but it's all for show.

True. I can't argue that. Still, you shouldn't have gone in alone. You had me worried.

Our gazes meet and hold for the first time all day. It's a calm moment until I take one step closer. He was already lying on the bed, half his sweatpant-covered ass hanging off the edge in an effort to fulfill my expectation that he act like a gentlemale.

As I approach, he almost falls off the edge with a pained groan.

"Damn! Do I reek? From my quick dash through the house?"

He nods.

I find clean t-shirts and pants and leave the porch, rounding the corner to the side of the house to change my clothes. I put on three sets of clothes because it's chilly out here. At this rate, we'll need a trip to a laundromat in no time.

After joining him in bed, I hug my edge as conscientiously as he's hugging his.

"Do you need some extra layers from your duffle? It's pretty cold here."

I look down as my phone pings. *"No, thanks. Orcs run hot."*

Well, damn, add that to my growing orc fantasy.

"I'm dead tired, Thornn. I have no idea how we're going to manage to muck out the house with it reeking as badly as it does, but I'm too fatigued to care. We'll talk in the morning."

Then, instead of falling right to sleep, which is what I had every intention of doing, I'm wide awake.

Really, how could I expect anything different? We may be hugging the edges of this six-foot-wide bed, but the more I get to know Thornn, the more handsome he gets. How many nights are we going to share this bed before we wake up in a huddle?

CHAPTER EIGHT

T hornn

Maybe it was the stress of being in such close quarters with someone I barely know, perhaps it was the long day, or possibly my visceral reaction to the heinous smell emanating from the house. For whatever reason, I managed to sleep through sunrise.

When I turn to look at Sarah, her side of this odd, round bed is empty. I reach for my phone on the floor to scold her for going back into the house without telling me, only to discover a text from her.

Believe it or not, a local figured out how to make a high-altitude bagel recipe. They're better than most of what you can find in L.A. I'm bringing back an assortment along with two kinds of schmears.

She must have assumed I don't know what a schmear is because she adds, *For the uninitiated, that's flavored cream cheese. I'm also stopping at the hardware store for every type of respirator they carry. If one of them doesn't work, perhaps we'll wear them all, one on top of the other. Also, I've come up with a plan of attack.*

I reply, *I'll have you know that Chief Brokka's mate, Marissa, loves bagels and brings them to the firehouse all the time. If it's not too late, put me down for a few everything bagels and some lox schmear—I'm a fan.*

Be there soon. I already have just what you want.

Just what I want? I doubt that. Just what I want would be a private jet back to the Zone.

Then it strikes me. That's not what I want. Sure, I'd like the house to magically clean itself, but being with Sarah isn't exactly torture.

Because the bed is round, not square, we gravitated to the middle where our legs could stretch out. I woke sometime around three in the morning with Sarah's hand on my chest and her legs tangled in mine. My cock was hard enough to hammer nails before I even swam back to consciousness.

I've always considered myself a good person, but before I backed away from her, I spent a moment taking her measure. She went from pretty to beautiful as she was bathed in the silvery moonlight filtering in through the screens.

It took all my self-control not to swipe away the strand of hair that was caught on her lips. I wanted to do more than that. My hands itched to caress her, explore her. Then the memories of everything I lost in that Purist attack hit me like a sledgehammer. I'm not a complete male anymore. No good for anyone, not at the firehouse, or with friends, and definitely not with a female—orc or human.

That was all the reminder I needed to roll over, slam my lids shut, and force myself back to sleep. Besides, even without all my inadequacies, there's no reason a woman like Sarah: pretty, rich, and smart enough to be working on her doctorate—would want to slum with an orc. Especially an orc like me.

I'm brought back to the present when I hear her car on the gravel. I jump out of bed, take a deep breath, and hurry to the front of the house to help her carry her purchases to the back porch.

It was dark last night with only a sliver of moonlight to illuminate the way. It's only now that I realize how beautiful it is here. We're surrounded by pines, with a few deciduous trees losing their leaves in the chill fall air. The mountains are already

CHAPTER EIGHT 35

snowcapped, though there's no snow on the ground here. The sky actually looks different here than it did in L.A., though I don't know how that's possible. I'd bet money on the fact that it's bluer.

When I see Sarah trying to juggle all her purchases, I jog to the car and try to slip everything she bought into my arms.

"I haven't had Mountain Man bagels in a decade, Thornn. You'll have to pry these out of my cold, dead hands." She snatches the brown paper bag back with a laugh.

When we're on the back porch, I impatiently watch as she opens a dozen napkins and lays them over the bed's white canvas covering.

Seems like a fool's errand, I text.

"No, it's not. I don't want to have to sleep on a bed of poppy seeds tonight."

That's why the Goddess invented the wind, I snark.

The smell of garlic from the everything bagels reminds me I'm starving. I can't wait for her to open the brown paper bag, so I begin eating one without benefit of schmear.

She tosses me a guilty look and admits, "I was starving. Did you really expect me not to scarf down the thirteenth bagel of the baker's dozen while I was driving?"

I've only had the one kind of bagels that Marissa brings, but I must agree these are the best I've ever tasted.

"Okay, here's what I'm thinking," Sarah says as she licks the cream cheese off her fingers.

I'm glad she brought plenty of napkins because my body likes the way her pointed pink tongue is capturing every last bit of cream cheese. After placing an unfolded napkin over my eager cock, I give her my full attention.

"I bought these." She fans out five different types of masks, respirators, and several tubs of menthol vapor rub. "I know you're supersensitive, but between the house airing out all night and a couple of these respirators, I'm hoping you can tolerate at least short stints inside."

She pulls out yet another napkin, but this has writing on it.

"I did this while I was waiting in line at Mountain Man."

The napkin has a sketch of both the main and second floors. As a pointer, she uses the white plastic knife that came with the cream cheese. She lays out her plan of attack: kitchen first, then the rest of the main floor.

"We'll get as much shit out to the roll-off in the front yard as quickly as possible. Hopefully, we'll find the offending substances sooner rather than later. Until we do, we'll keep working our way through the mess."

I still haven't been inside farther than the threshold.

How bad is it?

"It was dark last night. Because I was in such a hurry, I only took the time to flick on a few light switches. From what I saw, though, the short answer is: the house is completely full of shit except for goat paths. I read up on hoarding the day before we left. Really bad hoardy houses are so full of stuff, there are only paths through the junk. The proper term is actually 'goat paths'."

Shit.

"Yeah. You can put some exclamation points after that. Hopefully, her washer and dryer work. We can wash some blankets to sleep under. Hopefully, in a day or two, the kitchen will be usable."

I'm feeling overwhelmed and I haven't even seen the inside of the house.

"I imagine if we were in L.A., you'd quit about now, huh?"

She's right. The thought has certainly crossed my mind. But I haven't felt this... normal in a long time. At least all my inadequacies aren't staring me right in the face. I have something else to be focused on.

Good thing we're a thousand miles away, right? I'm stuck here.

I'm stuck here. And she's stuck with me.

CHAPTER NINE

Sarah

"Ready to suit up and head in?" I ask with forced cheerfulness.

Thornn gives me a wry look and a shrug.

As I help him adjust the straps on his heavy-duty respirator, I wonder what sent my aunt over the edge.

From my brief dive on the Internet, it sounds as though people often descend into the worst of their OCD after some type of trauma. Maybe it started when her husband died and she kept it under control until I was about ten, when she went all the way off the deep end. At any rate, I can see why our visits were always on vacation and not at her house.

Pushing open the back door releases another foul wave. Thornn gags, the filters doing little to cut the stench. I squeeze his arm in solidarity before leading the way to the first room, the kitchen.

We travel along the narrow path edged by teetering piles of decaying newspapers and magazines interspersed with layers of garbage. I flinch as something skitters away deeper into the mess. Oh geez, we're going to find all kinds of creatures in here.

"My next foray into town will include an extensive trip down the extermination aisle at the hardware store."

One of the stacks of newspapers only comes as high as my chin, which makes it easy to read the date.

CHAPTER NINE 39

"Dear God, this paper is ten years old. When did she think she was going to read it, after hell froze over? You doing okay?"

He nods halfheartedly, then pulls out his phone to text, *Maybe I'm getting used to it?*

"Who knows? Uh, I probably should have mentioned this earlier..."

His head swivels to look at me head-on, perhaps knowing that what's coming next isn't going to be good.

"Aunt Beth told me there were hidden gems and bearer bonds in here."

The poor orc's amber eyes go wild. I doubt it's about the possibility of a treasure hunt. It's probably at the thought of paging through a decade's worth of newspapers and magazines.

With the initial shock over, I inspect what I can see. Dirty, moldy dishes fill the sink and litter every inch of counter space. How did she cook in here? My gaze lands on a hot plate balanced precariously on a mini fridge lying on its side.

"Shit. Her stove was piled with so much junk she used a hot plate. So sad."

Thornn makes a noise behind his mask, a combination of clearing his throat and gagging.

"Maybe start with bagging the trash?" I suggest. "Get the worst of the smell contained?"

He gives me a thumbs up, already grabbing Hefty bags from the box I left just outside the back door.

"Put all reading material in the white bags I brought. Trash in the black. Black will go to the roll-off. White to the front porch. When we can't stay indoors for another second, I'll look through the white bags for the bonds."

He shakes his head, not in refusal, but in solidarity. No amount of respirators or plastic gloves are going to make this task tolerable.

I sort through the contents of the nearest counter. All food items, expired or not, go straight into the trash.

We work in silence except for the crinkling of bags and occasional clatter of glass bottles. The masks make talking a chore, but the steady activity keeps my mind off the monumental task ahead.

After girding my loins, I open the door to the surprisingly clean bathroom that opens off the kitchen. Just as I remember, not only is there a toilet and sink, but a shower and a modern washer and dryer. As luck would have it, there are sheets and towels in the hamper.

Still wearing my gloves—I'm no fool—I start a load as I envision hot showers for Thornn and myself when we're done slaving for the day.

Returning to the kitchen, I chance a glance at my helper. The sight of his muscular arms straining to contain overflowing bags of refuse sends an ill-timed flutter through my stomach. I scold myself after idly wondering if I'm developing a crush on the hired help. That's absurd, right? *Focus*, I scold myself, getting back to work.

By mid-morning, when we've cleared the kitchen counters and made a lot of headway on the kitchen floor, we take a breather outside. I hand Thornn his own box of sanitized wipes and a water bottle. "That was no joke. You hanging in there?"

He nods, chest heaving.

Over the next hours, we slowly clear everything out of the kitchen.

The oven was easy peasy, filled with clean pots and pans, but we've both avoided the fridge until the end.

"Ready for the fridge?" I ask.

He nods, the look on his face as full of determination as a warrior about to go into battle against an army that outnumbers him.

CHAPTER NINE 41

It's actually not that bad. The food went straight into black bags and the mold was dealt with rather easily with bleach and elbow grease. I don't know how we got so lucky, but the appliance is a new, stainless model. Looking around, I think we'll actually be able to cook in here.

My shoulders and back ache fiercely by the time we call it a day. I try not to dwell on how much more there is to sort and scrub, and I definitely don't want to think about the piles of white bags with my name on them waiting on the front porch.

One room down, Thornn texts when we've used dozens of antiseptic wipes and are sitting on the back porch. *How many to go?*

I grab the napkins I drew on while waiting at the bagelry, then count the rooms.

"Seventeen."

His amber eyes widen, mouth opens, and he holds a hand up to keep me from saying another word. Then he flops back on the bed with a groan.

Should I consider it a win that the groan almost qualifies as a word?

CHAPTER TEN

Thornn

"One benefit of Aunt Beth being a hoarder is that there were plenty of dirty clothes in the laundry area."

I don't know how, but she manages a smile even after all of today's backbreaking labor.

"I've done several loads between everything else today. We've got enough clean towels for both of us and I managed to wash and dry a quilt. Lucky us. I'm going to take a shower, then dine on bagels. Tomorrow I'll go to town again and get real food to fill our clean fridge."

I can smell a stream out back. I'm going to take a bath there, I text.

"You're not going to be too cold?"

Who knows? I might enjoy it.

I leave her in the house, hurry through the back porch, and burst out the back door. Following my nose toward fresh water, the smells and sounds of the outdoors hit me full force.

The crisp mountain air fills my lungs, scented with pine, damp leaves, and woodsmoke. Somewhere nearby, a stream burbles over rocks. An owl hoots. This is nothing like the city I've known my whole life.

CHAPTER TEN

I pull off my filthy clothes in a rush, leaving them scattered behind me in a trail. Completely naked, I run down the slope and into the forest, pine needles and twigs crunching under my bare feet.

It doesn't take me long to spot the stream, glinting silver in the twilight gloam. Without hesitation, I wade in up to my thighs, gasping at the icy bite. Scooping up handfuls of the clear water, I rub it over my arms and chest, and through my hair. The frigid temperature is exhilarating after so many hours sealed up with the reek of the house.

As I float on my back, gazing up at the limitless night sky strewn with glittering stars, something primal stirs deep inside me. This is how my orc ancestors must have lived, connected to the elements—the earth, wind, trees, and water.

We arrived on this planet through means we still don't understand. The elders who made the trip as adults talk at gatherings, educating us about the ways of our people, the ways of our past. Others have been caged in the Zone for decades now, severed from our roots, but this landscape calls to me as if it's imprinted on my very genes.

I've awakened to sensations and longings I've never known before. The freedom, the connection to nature, the solitude. For the first time since the attack, I don't feel broken or inadequate. Here, in nature, under the moonlight, I feel whole.

CHAPTER ELEVEN

Sarah

I thought I'd toweled my hair dry enough after my shower, but now, cuddled under the thick quilt in the bed on the porch, I'm shivering. My damp locks feel like icicles against my neck. I grab the towel and vigorously rub, trying to chase away the chill.

I'm not surprised when I check my phone and find no message from my parents. They'll be irritated that I left them out of the loop on this, but what was I supposed to do, send a carrier pigeon?

I'm huffing in annoyance when Thornn literally rises out of the mist hovering over the lawn. It's like something out of a movie—his huge, muscular jade figure materializing through the fog. I hear his footsteps first, twigs snapping underfoot. Then he's there, emerging as if in slow motion, steam rising off his nude body in the cool night air.

I'd already realized he was handsome, but seeing him like this, he's perfection. *Nude* perfection. Tree trunk thighs, shoulders wide enough to play football without pads, abs so ripped they look carved. His muscular arms hang loose at his sides, water droplets tracking down his skin. My mom would call him an Adonis. She wouldn't be wrong. Except he's not sculpted from marble, he's hewn from living jade.

His swirling tattoos are symmetrical, covering the top of his chest and full sleeves on both arms. I don't normally like tats, but on him? They accentuate his masculinity.

CHAPTER ELEVEN 45

As a doctoral candidate, I know it's important to gather thorough data. So I let my gaze travel over every inch of him, purely in the name of academic observation. And if my focus lingers a bit too long in certain areas, well, that's just being thorough.

Like on his cock. Even soft, it's still impressively long and thick, slapping lightly against his inner thighs as he walks. My friend Cherie, who used to sleep over when we were teenagers, used the term "man meat." It seemed so scandalous then, making us collapse into giggles. But I'm not laughing now as I admire the ample display before me. The visual sears into my mind.

I was so focused on his sex, I almost failed to notice the deep emerald scar slicing across his midsection. My lips purse in anger as I assume that was another present he received the day the hateful Purists attacked.

His towel is folded on his side of the bed. His shed clothing lies scattered across the lawn in a line toward the stream, forlorn little lumps of fabric dotting the overgrown grass. I finally tear my eyes away and turn my head in the other direction before he catches me gawking.

The screen door slams as he comes inside. I hear the sounds of him toweling dry and rummaging in his duffel for clean clothes. Then the mattress dips as he slides under the covers next to me. I sense his warmth along my back, even with a few inches still separating us. My phone dings with an incoming text.

Sorry. Sorry if I made you uncomfortable. Nudity is different for Others. I forgot humans aren't as comfortable as we are with it. Won't happen again.

The playful Thornn I joked with while we cleaned might have tolerated some gentle ribbing. If that version of him was here instead of this contrite version, I might teasingly tell him I enjoyed the show. But realizing he probably feels terrible over this perceived blunder, I say gently, "No problem. You were out there a while. I guess the cold didn't bother you too much?"

Cold, yes. But it felt good to be in nature. Not much of that in the Zone.

I've been on countless trips with my family, several to Europe. We went on driving trips a couple of summers. By my count, I've traveled to twenty-eight states. For a moment, I consider what it would be like to have never left the ten-block Integration Zone. It's mind-boggling what we did and continue to do to the Others.

Changing the direction of my thoughts, we chat for a few minutes. As I tell him goodnight, visions of a flawless, virile orc continue dancing behind my closed eyelids. His missing tusk, instead of being a detractor, only adds to his roguish appeal—at least in my fantasies.

As I imagine its jagged edge tracing down my fevered skin, I wonder what it would feel like—rough or smooth? Is it sharp enough to sting? To slide deliciously along my flesh? Somehow, I know the answer is yes. It would be sexy. Dangerously, addictively sexy.

I squeeze my thighs together against the swell of desire, but sleep remains elusive for a long time.

CHAPTER TWELVE

Thornn

The scent of pine fills my lungs as another crisp mountain dawn greets me. I stretch slowly, reluctant to leave the cozy nest of blankets and Sarah's warmth. Over the past week working side-by-side, her nearness has become a comfort I crave, though I know it's foolish. She's human, I'm an orc.

There are now a few human females mated to orc firefighters living in the Zone, but those males are worthy. They aren't broken. I am.

Even if I deserved her, which I don't, it could never be. I haven't come across kindness like hers from humans very often. But she could never be interested in me as a male. Even if I were human, there are things about me that, if she knew, would make her run in the other direction.

I glance at her to watch her sleep. It's a new frustrating, self-imposed pastime. Her chestnut hair is fanned over one of the pillows she bought. She's so peaceful and lovely it makes my heart squeeze. I force myself from the bed before I do something stupid like stroke a finger down her cheek.

We've cleared much of the main floor in the past seven days. The kitchen is functional, and the rented industrial-sized air purifiers Sarah had delivered are doing a good job, so the pungent odors are dissipating. Other rooms still overflow with mountains of trash, but each day the mansion feels more livable.

Only one thing remains the same—the frustrating silence imprisoning my voice. Around Sarah I feel words bubbling up, hovering on my lips, but they never pass the barrier. After forcing out the one word of 'thanks', I had hoped it would be the start of the dam breaking. Instead, the barricade feels stronger. I clench my jaw in anger at my mute impotence.

Though I feel powerless over my voice, my cock is far from unable to perform. Right now, just being inches away from her in bed, looking at her face, muscles slack and relaxed, has him hard as stone. Although I bathed in the stream last night, since there's only one place I have any privacy to take care of my erection, I feel the need for another trip to the water.

When Sarah wakes, I show her my phone screen: *Heading to the stream for a bath.*

"No problem. I'll start breakfast."

The frigid water is bracing from the autumn chill. I dunk below the surface, holding my breath, then burst up with a roar I can only voice here in solitude. If not for the attack, I'd be back in L.A. fighting fires and saving lives alongside my crew. Instead, I'm here, muzzled and unable to do the one thing in life that makes me feel worthwhile. Well, that's not exactly true. Helping Sarah feels rewarding, though the process is stinky.

By the time I return, Sarah has bagels and fruit laid out on the little wooden table we carried into the sun and bleached to within an inch of its life. We eat quickly, both impatient to resume work. The sooner we finish, the sooner I can escape these confusing feelings about my lovely, off-limits boss.

We've done most of the rooms on the main floor, but saved the large parlor for last. It's filled with bookshelves and knickknacks. In here, Sarah hopes to find some of the treasure she's searching for. It's slow going as we page through every book and inspect every cranny of every memento.

Around noon, Sarah checks her phone and makes an announcement. "I'm going into town at five. I know you want to avoid people, but I'd like you to come with me."

CHAPTER TWELVE

My eyes narrow as my suspicions rise. *Where are you taking me?*

She shakes her head, lips pursed to hold back her secret. "It's a surprise."

My hands fist as anxiety and irritation war inside me.

I don't like surprises. And I don't want to go into town.

Her forehead bunches and her lips twist. I guess she's readying herself for a debate.

"I think if I tell you, you'll refuse. But if you just give it a chance, I think you'll like the idea."

By the sincere look on her face, it's clear this is important to her, but the idea of being in a sea of humans makes my guts clench. I don't even text her a response. I simply shake my head as I spear her with my most serious gaze.

She heaves a long sigh, then spills her secret. "Okay, okay. I made an appointment for you to see a dentist." Putting her hands up in a don't-shoot motion, she explains, "I talked to Dr. Goldberg and explained your situation. She was unbelievably nice. She heard of the Others landing in the desert when she was a teenager and is excited to meet you. She offered to see you after regular working hours, and even suggested we park in the rear lot to enter through her back door. She'll take a look. See if she can make a cap or an implant for your tusk."

Rage boils up. How dare she interfere, make decisions for me without asking? Go behind my back and reach out to someone without my permission? She knows nothing of what I've suffered. I turn away so she won't see the bitterness distorting my face.

Her voice comes softly from behind. "I'm sorry, Thornn. I just thought... maybe if we can replace or repair your tusk, help you feel more whole again, it might help give you the confidence to speak. Kam mentioned how important tusks are to orcs, that they're part of your identity. I wanted to give you more than an hourly wage. I considered this a present."

The genuine remorse in her words deflates my anger. I realize then her gesture comes from caring about me, not pity or presumption. And I desperately want my tusk back, the visible reminder of my stolen masculinity. Amelia, my friend Thrall's human mate who is a social worker, tried to find a dentist who would fix the tusk, but no one she called wanted to work on an Other. Still, after so many months of disappointments, I don't dare hope. But for Sarah, I'll try.

CHAPTER THIRTEEN

Sarah

I grip the steering wheel tightly as we pull into the rear parking lot of Dr. Goldberg's office. Guilt and doubt plague me. Who am I to make this decision for Thornn without asking him first? Yet my intentions come from a place of caring. I want to help restore his confidence and identity.

As I put the car in park, I chance a glance at his stoic profile. His jaw is clenched, fingers laced tightly in his lap. Reaching over, I give his arm a gentle squeeze.

"I know you're nervous and I can't promise this will be a magic fix. But please know I care about you very much and only want good things for you. Of course, the final choice is yours."

His taut expression softens a bit, and he nods. As we walk toward the back door the doctor said would be unlocked, I'm hyper-aware of his tension. After we enter through the plain metal door into a nondescript hallway, my sneakers squeak across the linoleum floors. At the end, I give my name to the petite, silver-haired receptionist. Her kindly features show almost no reaction to Thornn's imposing presence. Dr. Goldberg must have given her advanced warning.

"Right this way." She leads us to an office and gestures Thornn toward the exam chair. Dr. Goldberg enters, white coat swishing. Her keen brown eyes assess Thornn from behind stylish cat-eye glasses.

She shakes his hand warmly. "So very nice to meet you, Thornn. Sarah explained your situation, and I'd be happy to take a look at that tusk of yours."

Over the next few minutes, her calm competence seems to put Thornn more at ease. She examines the jagged stump and then explains the choices. When I ask about a crown, which I assumed would be the best option, the doctor considers for a while, then shakes her head.

"It's such a big piece of real estate—ivory real estate. From the front, the piece looks smooth, but the back is jagged and broken off much closer to the gum line. I don't think a crown would be sturdy enough."

She punches info into her computer and rotating 3D models appear on her computer screen. Thornn leans forward with interest.

"The process will take several steps over the next couple of months," she explains. "First, I'll take an impression of your mouth as well as detailed scans and images. I'll create a 3D model of your mouth and craft the prosthetic. That will take two to three weeks."

Thornn's gaze flashes to me in worry, but the doctor doesn't seem to notice. She continues to explain the process.

"If it wasn't the close of business, I could extract your tusk and insert the screw into your jaw today. But I just happened to have a cancellation Friday at one if you want. It's an extraction, then an incision into the bone to insert the screw. You'll only need a local anesthetic. The surgery takes about an hour. No heavy lifting for the rest of the day. After that, you'll need to let it heal for 4-6 weeks before we attach the final prosthetic tusk."

As she pulls off her gloves, she explains, "Healing times vary. We can evaluate based on your progress. Attaching the tusk is painless, just some adhesive and minor adjustments. From start

CHAPTER THIRTEEN   53

to finish, if all goes smoothly, we're looking at two to three months. But I'm optimistic you'll have an excellent outcome."

Thornn pulls out his phone, types his question, and flashes it at the doctor.

I won't be here in three months.

"Sarah said you're from L.A.? I went to school with a Dr. Harding who practices in Santa Monica. We sometimes see each other at periodontal conferences. I can implant the post before you leave. I have an amazing woman who will make the actual implant. She's an artist—literally. Just does this to keep her cash flow coming in. She'll match the color perfectly for you, then we'll send it to Dr. Harding, who can do the final implantation."

She rolls her chair back and gives Thornn a warm smile.

"This will work, Thornn. Just say yes, and I'll contact Dr. Harding to make sure he's available. I can make the impression before you leave today."

Thornn's eyes shine brighter and the tension in his shoulders unwinds as he nods his approval. Then his happiness disappears faster than autumn leaves in a gust of wind.

He types a question to the doctor, shows it to her, and she answers with a number that makes the strong orc sitting beside me gasp in shock. He must have asked how much the procedure costs.

He shakes his head sadly and texts Dr. Goldberg. This time I read the words on his screen, *Thank you so much, but I can't afford it.*

As he rises to leave, I interrupt. "I knew how much this was going to cost, Thornn. I wouldn't have brought you here if I didn't intend to pay for it. Consider it a bonus."

The doctor rises and says, "I've got a few emails to respond to. I'll let you hash this out and return in a few minutes."

Thornn and I proceed to have one of our odd half-spoken, half-text arguments. By the time Dr. Goldberg returns, his screen reads, *Okay. You pay, but at the end of this job, I will pay you back out of what you owe me.*

I know how limited his funds are and am happy to pay, but the male has lost enough self-esteem for a lifetime. If he feels such a strong need to pay for this, I'll let him.

This strong, resilient male has endured so much hardship. My heart swells to see a glimmer of hope taking root inside him. However difficult the road ahead, this first step feels as though it was meant to be.

CHAPTER FOURTEEN

Thornn

The late afternoon sun glints off the hood of Sarah's Subaru as we make our way down the mountain toward her aunt's mansion. I lean forward and deliberately place my phone in the glove compartment, the significance of the gesture hitting me fully.

Ever since the attack, my phone has been my security blanket, my only means of communication. Setting it aside feels momentous, like I'm shedding the past and embarking on a new journey.

Sarah glances at me, one brow quirked in surprise. "Everything okay?"

I nod, clearing my throat. My voice is dry as brittle leaves as I force out, "Yeah." I pause, cough, and try again. "Thank... you." Two words shouldn't feel like summiting Everest, but difficult as that was, triumph lights me up inside.

Her lovely features soften into a blinding smile. "You're so welcome, Thornn."

I breathe deeply, drawing in her sweet floral scent mingled with the pine air wafting through the partially cracked windows.

My tongue feels thick and clumsy in my mouth, but I force myself to say more. "Future. See it... now." Frustration wars with determination. Jaw clenched, I force out another fractured phrase. "You... helped me."

Sarah blinks back sudden tears, though her tone stays gentle. "I'm happy to help however I can."

We've worked side by side for a week. Certainly I knew she wanted me to speak, but I hadn't realized how deeply my effort would touch her. She doesn't just want to talk to me so I can perform like a trained monkey as we muck out the house. It strikes me how much she wants to communicate with me—to connect.

I force my gaze forward, knowing if I look at her too long, I'll drown in her summer blue eyes. I long to tell her more of how I feel, but speaking even in short bursts leaves me shaken. Still, making the effort fills me with pride. Sarah just listens, focused wholly on me, as I string together a few more stilted words during the drive.

"This place... good for me," I rasp, gesturing at the forest flying by outside the window as the back of my mind rejoices at the benchmark of saying five words in a row.

Sarah nods. "I think so too. The mountain air suits you." She gives me a playful sideways glance. "And I won't complain about the view when you go bathing in the stream."

I feel my cheeks flush emerald. How odd that for the first time in my life I'm embarrassed by my nudity. Clearing my throat, I change the subject. "House... making headway."

"We've got a week or two of mucking out the junk, then there are all the white bags on the porch as I look for buried treasure. We've made incredible progress, though." Sarah reaches across the gearshift and squeezes my hand. "I couldn't have done it without you, Thornn."

I turn my hand so our fingers thread together. She doesn't pull away, instead she gives a gentle squeeze.

CHAPTER FOURTEEN 57

Her skin is petal soft against my rough, work-worn palm. The contact sends tingles up my arm. I cling to her hand like a lifeline as we chat about the remainder of tasks at the mansion. Focusing on our joined fingers helps ease my anxiety about forcing out words.

Later, as we prepare for bed on the porch, Sarah gifts me an approving smile. "I'm proud of you, Thornn."

Hearing those words in her musical voice makes all the struggle worthwhile. Hope burns inside me for the first time in forever.

CHAPTER FIFTEEN

Sarah

We stopped for fast food on the way home. After a week of bagels and frozen dinners, a Whopper tasted like fine dining.

Since we already took our showers before our trip to the dentist, getting ready for bed is a quick affair. I perform a mental review of the last few hours. Of course, I'm thrilled he allowed himself to get the implant, and even more excited about our discussion on the way home in the car. Having a real conversation with him felt even better than I'd expected.

But right now, as I slide under the thick quilt on our shared bed, I keep replaying his response when I said I appreciated the view of him naked. He blushed. Well... I assume his turning the prettiest shade of emerald was a blush. But he didn't protest. He kept his grip firmly on my hand.

Even though I tend to freeze at night, he sleeps only in sweatpants. I assume the pants are for my benefit, because the male puts off enough warmth to heat half the mountain. Just knowing he's inches away from me with all that luscious green skin and all those hard, firm, tantalizing muscles has been cutting into my sleep time.

CHAPTER FIFTEEN 59

I've been fighting my attraction to him for days and could debate with myself for another week about whether he'll welcome a kiss, but the only way to know for sure is to try.

After our emotional intimacy this evening, I decide I can't wait one more day to do what I've been fantasizing about for days.

It will get really awkward if he turns me down, but I just don't have the self-control to hold back.

I turn onto my side, propping myself up on one elbow, fully intending to caress that handsome face with my fingertips and brush my lips temptingly over his. My tentative courage evaporates when I realize his breathing has shifted, becoming deep and even.

I huff a disappointed sigh. He's sound asleep. Our long day must have worn him out—the strenuous work at the house, the stress of our trip into town, and the emotional upheaval of visiting the dentist's office. I could see how much effort it took for him to speak. That was a monumental breakthrough for what I assume a professional would label his PTSD.

Flopping onto my back, I cross my arms like a petulant child denied a treat. I'm the one who pushed for the implant. I should be more understanding about his exhaustion. But now my nerve has fled, and I'll probably obsess all night, wrestling with whether I dare try to kiss him tomorrow.

Trying to settle my frustration, I take comfort in his nearness, his solid warmth mere inches away. The comforting weight of his big body dipping the bed and the earthy scent of him soothes me toward slumber.

As I drift off, fantasies play through my mind—leaning into his strength, running my hands over sleek muscle and smooth jade skin. I imagine his arms enfolding me as his full lips claim mine, fierce yet achingly tender.

I wake slowly, blinking against the gray dawn light filtering through the porch screens. A smile tugs at my lips as I bask in delicious sensations—the press of a powerful male body against my back, his sculpted chest and abs molded to my curves. My head cradled on his biceps, his other arm wrapped firmly around my waist. Our legs are tangled together and my bottom is pressed intimately against his groin.

My breath catches at the unmistakable rigid length nestled against my backside—impressive even at rest. Sweet arousal unfurls inside me. Apparently, sleepy Thornn isn't as immune to my nearness as stoic waking Thornn pretends to be.

Snuggling closer, I inhale his woodsy scent mingled with the clean cotton sheets. With my head on his arm, it's easy to steal a kiss there. It's not even a kiss, really, just a soft brush of my lips over his skin. He makes a rough sound low in his throat that vibrates through me, igniting my nerve endings like sparklers. My body thrums with awakening hunger.

His arm tightens around me as he burrows closer. Is he awake? Asleep? If he's sleeping, when he wakes up, will he pull away? I gasp when he presses an open-mouthed kiss to the sensitive spot beneath my ear. My back arches, my nipples pebbling against the t-shirt I wore to bed as I picture what he's doing with his thick, black tongue.

Heart pounding, I twist in his embrace. Through the silvery predawn light, I read desire darkening his amber eyes before they drift closed. He eases toward me, achingly slowly, perhaps to see if I'll pull away. I stand my ground, a clear message as he claims my mouth in a searing kiss that steals my breath even as it makes me throb with wanting.

The velvet heat of his lips plays over mine, coaxing rather than demanding. When the wet tip of his tongue traces the seam of my mouth, I open eagerly with a pleading whimper. As our tongues dance and twine, sweet tension coils ever tighter inside me.

His hand cups my face, thumb caressing along my jawbone, callused fingertips sending shivers down my spine. Running my hands up his hard chest, I marvel at the contrast of steel muscles and velvet skin.

CHAPTER FIFTEEN 61

I press a kiss to the dip in his collarbone where it must have been broken at some time in the past. His skin is fever-hot, his muscles like iron cords under taut green skin.

Bending lower, I brush my lips over the hills and valleys of his chest until I arrive at the scar that travels from one side of his chest to the other. In the dim dawn light, it's such a deep emerald it's almost black. My heart aches to think of him outnumbered and helpless, fighting for survival.

I trace along it in one smooth pass, then reverse directions and drop a dozen tiny kisses along it. Does he feel my affection? Does he know how fervently I wish I could heal him with my touch?

Slowly, my hands venture lower, over the swell of his defined abs until my fingertips graze the waistband of his low-slung pants. His erection presses against it, straining for release.

Although my body is ramping up, I don't want to take this all the way. Not right now. It's too much, too soon. Perhaps he feels it too, the need to enter this delicate relationship more slowly. He nudges me upward so he can nuzzle my neck. His broken tusk grazes my collarbone as his mouth trails down my throat, tongue flicking the sensitive spot below my ear.

Soft whimpers escape me as he re-claims my mouth, his tongue delving deeper, urgent and demanding now. I wrap my arms around his broad shoulders, digging my short nails into his rock-hard back.

"Thornn," I gasp, his name ending on a moan.

He growls low in his chest, the rumble reverberating through me and straight to my core. My chest is rising and falling so rapidly the t-shirt clings to my breasts, damp with perspiration. In this position, there is no escaping his heated gaze as it travels over every inch of me.

"I want you," he rumbles against my skin, every growled word like a caress to my already over-sensitive body. "So bad it burns."

Just when I'm about to climb on top of all that hard muscle and take what I crave, his eyes fly open and he shakes his head. I glimpse what might be horror or remorse before he turns away from me with a tortured groan. The loss of his touch leaves me bereft.

"Sorry... shouldn't have..." He rakes a hand through his rumpled waves. "You deserve more... better..." Avoiding my eyes, he rolls off the bed and stalks off the porch toward the trees, muscular back rigid as he jogs toward the stream.

I curl my empty arms around my chest, kiss-swollen lips tingling. My body throbs for his, but stronger by far is the ache in my heart. Something wounded and haunted lurks behind his self-protective barriers. Something tells me his rejection is about more than his mangled tusk.

Whatever secret pain Thornn carries, I yearn to soothe and comfort him. But first, he has to let me in.

CHAPTER SIXTEEN

T hornn

Fuck! How did I let myself get carried away like that?

Well, the answer to that is obvious. I've developed feelings for Sarah. She's smart, pretty, and kind. And willing. No matter how many times I replay what just happened in our bed, I can't convince myself she was repelled by my kisses. In fact, I'm almost certain she's the one who started our passionate encounter.

I tear off my sweats the moment I near the stream and wade in hastily, gasping as the frigid water envelops my thighs. Good. The bitter chill is a welcome distraction, swiftly subduing my earlier arousal. However, it does little to calm the storm of emotions raging within me.

By the Goddess, why did that have to be the best kiss of my life? Fate seems determined to torment me—not only am I powerfully attracted to Sarah, but I genuinely admire and care for her. Out of all the females I could develop feelings for, why did it have to be this one? The one who stirs my heart as much as my body? It would be so much simpler if my interest was merely physical.

I'm a formidable male—tall, muscular, and strong. Without hesitation, I charged into a mob of Purist thugs to protect my friends. Routinely, I rush into burning buildings when everyone else is fleeing. So how is it that I retreated from our passionate embrace this morning like a coward?

Of course I know the reason why. The memory is etched into my mind as indelibly as the scars marring my flesh. That night of the riot, I lost more than my braids and half a tusk to those Purist bastards. I lost a testicle as well.

Even now, the shame and devastation of it threaten to choke me. What happens when gentle, affectionate Sarah reaches between my legs and discovers I'm half a male? Damaged goods. Her revulsion and disappointment will shred me to ribbons inside. I can picture her pretty face transforming with dawning horror and pity. Just the thought makes me want to roar out my anguish.

There were so many attackers that night. Several came at me with knives. One slashed across my chest, another stabbed my thigh.

A kick from behind just missed my kidney but broke three ribs. I went down. It must have been a steel-toed boot that kicked me in the face, cracking my jaw and breaking my tusk. A stomp on my chest broke my collarbone and two more ribs. The one who cut me grabbed my hair in his fist with the bloody knife, and cut off what he called my "girly braids." The brutal kick to my groin made me roar in agony. Then I blacked out.

The National Guard must have stopped the fight. They took me to the Zone Medical Center. The ruptured testicle had to be removed.

No one else knows the full extent of my injuries. Luckily, there was a substitute doctor at the clinic the night I was attacked. I swore the surgeon to secrecy, knowing he would never practice in the Zone again. Not even Marissa, Chief Brokka's mate who runs the local clinic, is aware of the barbaric blow I suffered.

As far as most are concerned, the loss of my hair and tusk during the attack is the reason for my extended silence. They understand—an orc's tusks represent his masculinity and pride. Orc males never cut their hair. They may shave the sides, but the long braids are a symbol of strength. It will take long years to restore it to its former glory. If my friends knew those thugs unmanned me that night along with disfiguring me, I would never escape their sympathy and sorrow.

The Integration Zone has been my whole world. Although it covers ten city blocks, rumors spread with lightning swiftness. If one person discovers my shame, everyone will know within hours.

A small voice whispers that Sarah isn't part of the Zone social web. Even if she learns my secret, she has no one to tell.

Except she's friends with Emma, Kam's mate. And Kam, as much as I like him, cannot keep a secret. Once he knows, all the orcs in the Zone will know my humiliation.

Even if no Others learn my secret, Sarah will know, and her opinion, her reaction, is the most important of all. I couldn't bear to see the look in her eyes when she finds I'm only half a male.

I plunge below the surface of the icy stream, needing to shock my system back into balance. Breaking the surface with a roar I can only voice in solitude here in the wilderness, I know what I must do.

I'll work tirelessly over these next weeks to help Sarah clear out her aunt's estate. I'll redouble my efforts until we find whatever hidden riches she believes are squirreled away. And then I'll flee this place—and her—as swiftly as I can, retreating within the familiar boundaries of the Zone before my traitorous heart betrays me further.

I can't allow sweet Sarah to uncover the bitter truth—that I'm irrevocably broken, no longer a whole male. I'm doomed to live out my days silent and celibate, with the phantom ache of all I've lost as my sole companion. As much as it devastates me to abandon this unexpected chance at happiness, some secrets are too painful to reveal.

CHAPTER SEVENTEEN

Sarah

I wipe a layer of dust off the top of a massive leather-bound book and slide it back onto the shelf with a sneeze. My gaze travels down the soaring line of built-in bookcases that cover the entire rear wall of the parlor. The rich mahogany panels and elegant crown molding speak of bygone gracious living in this old Colorado mansion.

It's been two days since Thornn and I shared that steamy encounter in bed, followed by his abrupt, anguished departure. We've both pretended it never happened and have thrown ourselves into clearing the main floor with a vengeance.

Tension simmers beneath our polite interactions as we meticulously sort through endless piles of clutter. My body still tingles, recalling his kisses and the temptation of all that hard muscle pressed intimately against me. I constantly bite my tongue to keep from begging him to talk to me, to let me in.

One good thing has happened. He talks more every day. Unfortunately, our conversations are superficial. The emotional intimacy we had begun to share is just a memory.

As I reach for another book, my fingers brush against something smoother than aged leather. I grasp the small velvet bag and upend the contents onto my palm, gasping aloud at what spills

CHAPTER SEVENTEEN 67

out. An ornate emerald necklace with one large teardrop stone glitters in my hand alongside a single matching earring. My pulse leaps. This is the first piece of hidden treasure we've found. I wonder if the twin earring is hidden somewhere in this room.

"Thornn, come quick! I've found something!" My voice rings with breathless excitement.

Heavy footsteps pound down the hallway before Thornn skids to a stop in the doorway, chest heaving. His tawny gaze locks onto the jewelry in my upturned palm and his eyes widen. I hold it out with a triumphant grin.

"What do you think? Genuine emeralds?"

Reverently taking the offerings, he turns the gemstones in the light, enthralled. "I've never seen emeralds, but I doubt your aunt would have put them in that bag and hidden them if they were fakes."

His lips quirk upward, a hint of wonder piercing through his usually solemn demeanor. My chest fills with affection for this complex, vulnerable male. In this moment, with his defenses lowered, I glimpse the tender heart hidden behind his stoic armor.

Buoyed by the excitement of the moment, I can't resist standing on tiptoe to brush a swift kiss across his cheek. "Something tells me the other earring is here somewhere. Let's start hunting!"

Thornn blinks hard, but his tentative smile lingers. The easy camaraderie that has returned reminds me how much I've come to cherish his calm, quiet presence and the rare glimpses of his playful humor. Treasures aside, what I long to uncover most is the key to healing his wounded spirit.

We continue to search the nooks and crannies of the expansive bookcases, to no avail. Other than stirring up clouds of dust and signs of a past mouse infestation, our efforts yield nothing. I'm glad I made quick work of the rodents after a visit from the exterminator last week, so other than a few squeaks, that challenge seems behind us.

When afternoon sunlight filtering through the dusty bay window turns golden, I straighten with a frustrated sigh. As I lean backward, my hands bracing the small of my back, I say, "I need a break. Want me to throw together some sandwiches?"

Thornn nods, continuing to work on the top shelves of the bookcase as I pull ingredients from the fridge. Spreading mayo on slices of bread, my thoughts drift back to the charged encounter in our shared bed. I recall his blazing eyes and passionate kisses with vivid clarity.

I'm sure he must feel something for me. If the bed-kisses weren't proof enough, the heated way he gazed at me after I just pressed that impulsive kiss to his cheek hinted that his feelings are more than friendship. My nerve endings sizzle at the memories.

I set the knife down with resolve. The time for subtlety is over. I have two choices—find a way to seduce that stubborn male... or walk away before my heart becomes irreparably entangled.

"Soup's on," I call to him as I put our sandwiches on plates and set them on the table we've returned to the kitchen after bleaching it in the sun. I don't know about the second floor, not having braved a visit in days, but down here, the smell is tolerable.

Thornn wanders in, settles across from me, and tucks in as though he hasn't eaten in days.

My nerves jump as I blurt, "Do you feel anything for me beyond friendship?"

He pauses, mid-chew, but says nothing.

"Because I care for you." When he doesn't respond, I add, "More than as a friend or employee."

His dark amber eyes widen, but his jaw firms with resolve. "You deserve better."

I lean forward, grasping his hand even as he tries half-heartedly to pull away. "That's not what I asked. Stop trying to decide what's best for me and just tell me truthfully what you feel."

CHAPTER SEVENTEEN 69

He gazes at our joined hands, conflicted emotions playing over his face. "I'm attracted." His voice scratches at the admission. "A lot." By the way those words were torn from him, it's clear it cost him to admit it.

Triumph courses through me even as I play at being calm. "I hoped as much after... the other morning." I pierce him with my gaze, hoping by the sheer force of it he believes it's true.

His full lips flatten. "It was a mistake to lose control like that."

I relinquish the battle to rein in my frustration. "Why? Is it the differences between our species holding you back? Help me understand."

"Some things can't be fixed." His words are cryptic, his eyes hooded.

Sitting back, I cross my arms. "Can't fix *me*? *You*? What? If we're both interested, we can find a way to overcome just about anything. Look at Kam and Emma. They're making it work against all odds."

When remorse flashes across his face, I soften my tone. "I'm developing feelings for you, Thornn. Now that you're talking and I'm getting to know you, I've found so many things I like about you. There's just so much more I want to learn. I wish you would let me in."

His Adam's apple bobs, and I wonder if he's struggling to maintain his silence or to find the right words. But he simply repeats, "You deserve better. Far better than me."

Though we seem to be going in circles with more questions than answers, one certainty crystallizes—the heat in his eyes confirms that his desire equals mine. Despite his insistence that I deserve better, I vow to chip away at his defenses until he admits we should pursue this attraction.

I've always considered myself a down-to-earth person, level-headed, calm, a straight shooter. Well, goodbye strait-laced Sarah, and hello femme fatale. I'm going to seduce this orc or die trying.

CHAPTER EIGHTEEN

Thornn

How long can I go on like this? Desperately wanting Sarah with every breath I take, yet convinced I'm right about shutting my attraction down. It's one thing for me to control my own cravings, but Sarah is making no secret of her desire to take things further.

It must be close to bedtime. We usually knock off around five, but I'm still working, despite Sarah repeatedly urging me to take a break. Why would I do that? First of all, free time means there's nothing to do other than talk to Sarah, which only stirs us both up as we grow closer to each other by the hour. And second, the more I work, the faster we'll be done and the sooner we can drive back to Cali and never see each other again.

"Thornn?"

She's calling from the back porch again, subtly urging me to knock off for the day. I'll ignore her, keep inspecting every book and knickknack on these high shelves although my calves and thighs are aching from standing on this ladder for the last few hours.

"Thornn?"

Her voice is closer. She's in the room with me.

CHAPTER EIGHTEEN

"I thought I'd finish on the ladder before I knocked off for the night."

"Could you help me with something?"

I can ignore her and avoid her, but I can't resist helping her. When I swivel on the ladder to look at her, what I see steals my breath.

"Oh, fuck!"

My knees lock and I grip the edge of the wooden shelf. Sarah's standing in the wide doorway, naked as the day she was born.

The smile pasted on her face flickers for a moment as her lids fly wide, but she doesn't move.

"I... wanted to make my intentions clear. Didn't want any doubts about where I stand."

Where she stands is twelve feet away, without a stitch of clothing. Is she pausing for me to respond? I don't know what to say. My ability to think has flown away, leaving me tongue-tied, yet instantly horny.

"So, this is me making a statement. If you want to take our relationship to another level, I'm ready." Almost under her breath, she adds, "It's not every day I throw my naked body at a guy I'm interested in."

My boner is hard enough to dent metal, but my mind is swirling with three words on perma-repeat—she deserves better. I know she doesn't want to hear that, so I remain silent.

"Uh, this cost me, Thornn. It's a statement. If you're not interested, say red and I'll never bring it up again. Scout's honor. We can pretend this never happened and you'll never have to worry about a repeat performance."

"Red?" I'm having trouble following her words. She's so fucking beautiful. So sexy. So... Sarah. She could never pull off flirtatious—that's not who she is. It makes perfect sense that she'd just come at what she wants head-on. Direct, without being demanding.

"Red means halt. *No más.* Hard stop."

It's only when she says this that I realize stopping is the farthest thing from my mind. Look at her, she's like a nude in a classical painting with her full hips, rounded breasts, and wavy brown hair tumbling over her shoulders. How could anyone say no to what she's offering? The idea of why I've decided to refuse escapes me.

"If red means stop, then green means go?" I ask, though I hate myself for even entertaining the idea.

"Yeah. So what's your color, Thornn?" The moment has been so serious until now, but a little bubble of laughter escapes her. "Stupid question," she mumbles. "You're an orc."

I laugh with her as I say, "Green, Sarah. My skin is green and so am I."

She sighs in relief as she crosses the room, offering a hand to help me off the ladder. It suddenly strikes me how I can manage our intimate moments so that she won't discover my shameful secret. I don't know why I hadn't thought of it before. Perhaps my mind wasn't sufficiently motivated until she waltzed into the room naked.

The moment my feet hit the floor, she reaches to embrace me, her hands on my shoulders urging me lower so we can kiss. Mimicking her position with my arms on her shoulders, I extend my arms to full length, pushing our bodies apart.

"There's something I need to say." I hope the deep timbre of my voice telegraphs how serious I am.

I ease her backward to the wall left of the dining room doorway, then press her against it, my grip still keeping her at arm's length.

"What do you know about orcs in the bedroom?" I lean to put my face the same height as hers, moving in a bit closer than she might be comfortable with, to set the stage for what's to come.

CHAPTER EIGHTEEN

"Um... you're my first orc."

"Emma's your best friend. She never mentioned what she and Kam share in the bedroom?"

"We may be best friends, but on some topics, less is more."

"Then let me inform you that male orcs are dominant, Sarah. I guess it's a factor of evolution back on An'Wa. Female orcs are strong and fight back. Our relationships usually begin with a fight for supremacy. They always end with the male on top."

I raise my eyebrows to make sure she gets the picture.

"Okay. So... missionary position?"

Is she being purposely obtuse? Probably not. I'll spell it out.

"I will be in charge of all things in the bedroom. It's in my DNA, can't be changed. If you can't handle it, I suggest you be the one to say red. Now."

Her chin lifts and juts toward me. Is she balking already?

In all my life, I've never been so invested in hearing someone's answer. I want her to say green more than I've ever wanted anything in my entire life.

Chapter Nineteen

Sarah

My heartbeat is galloping and I'm panting as though I just ran a race. I wish I knew whether it was from fear or arousal. Probably both.

My nipples are puckered with need, and desire is swirling in my pelvis. That happened as I shucked my clothes a few minutes ago and then it ramped up as I walked into this room. What's happening now, though, is nothing like that.

My arousal is in the stratosphere, and I think it's from the way his eyes have a carnelian cast, burning from his own desire. Or maybe it's the way his cock is pulsing against his loose sweats, or how his gaze has moved from reading my facial expression to roving up and down my body.

I know the exact moment I went from aroused to on fire. It was the words 'I will be in charge in all things in the bedroom'. I never knew I was into that. Until now.

"Yellow."

He cocks his head in question. Although he's not speaking, I don't think this has anything to do with his mutism. He's asserting his dominance, wordlessly commanding me to expand on my answer.

CHAPTER NINETEEN

"Green for desire, red for no. So I'm yellow, for fear."

"Fear of what?" His tone is commanding.

Pausing, I examine my emotions, then tremble when I come upon the answer. I can't tell him the truth because the answer is that I'm afraid of how much I'm going to like this.

"Changed my mind. I'm green, Thornn. If I say red, you'll stop?"

"Red means halt. *No más*. Hard stop, Sarah. I'm hard-wired to be dominant, not a rapist. I'm in control until you say that one word. Then you're in charge."

"Okay." I catch his gaze and hold it, letting him know I agree. Then something deep inside my own DNA takes over and I lower my eyes, the prey acknowledging their submission to the predator.

My body hums with anticipation as Thornn turns me to face the wooden wall. The texture is cool and smooth against the delicate skin of my cheek, heightening the sensation of vulnerability.

Thornn's hands slide along my sides, sending shivers down my spine. I can't help but tense, my muscles coiling as his broken tusk brushes gently along the nape of my neck. It's a stark reminder of his otherness, and yet, it adds to the excitement coursing through me.

His lips descend on my neck, leaving a trail of scorching kisses that set my skin ablaze. Each touch is like wildfire, igniting the desire within me. Heat spreads, consuming me from the inside out.

He cups my breasts, his large palms encompassing them. The firmness of his touch sends a jolt of pleasure straight to my core. My nipples harden against his palms, begging for more attention.

His thumbs circle my pebbled peaks, sending waves of pleasure radiating throughout my body. I can't help but moan low from the back of my throat, the sound echoing in the almost empty room. His touch is both gentle and demanding, igniting a primal hunger within me that I didn't know existed.

"You are... the best surprise of my life," he husks into my ear. He seems to have no trouble talking now that he has me up against the wall. "I've wanted to do this since shortly after I met you. I don't know how I managed to control myself all this time."

Perhaps I'm the one who's now mute. My only response is a shaky exhalation as I arch my back to garner more of his touch.

His lips graze my neck, then trail down my spine in a line of featherlight kisses. Each touch leaves me wanting more, craving his touch on every inch of my skin. My body is a symphony of sensations, every nerve alive with desire.

Thornn's hands slide lower, caressing my hips before moving around to press the flat of his palm between my legs. He doesn't press a finger between my folds. In fact, I'm not sure this is meant to arouse me.

His possessiveness makes me throb with desire. I can't help but press myself against him, wanting to feel the hard planes of his body against mine, to capture even a graze of his hard cock against my flesh.

His breath tickles my ear as he whispers, his voice laced with desire, "You're mine, Sarah. Only mine."

His words send a thrill through me, stoking my fiery desire to new heights. I'm lost in the intensity of the moment, my body craving the dominance he offers. I arch and bend my knees, pressing myself harder into his palm, offering myself fully to him.

One thick finger slides along my folds. A gasp escapes my lips as he finds the wetness there, his touch setting off sparks of pleasure that shoot through me like lightning.

He doesn't hide his low rumble of approval as he teases me, his touch maddeningly light as he circles my entrance, never venturing inside. I'm on the verge of begging for more when he finally presses a finger inside me. The sensation of him

CHAPTER NINETEEN

breaching me is overwhelming, and I can't help but release a cry of startled enjoyment.

My body trembles with desire and I take a moment to realize I'm panting with need as Thornn's finger delves deeper inside me. I'm overwhelmed by the sensations coursing through my veins, the way his touch sets my skin ablaze and sends shockwaves of pleasure straight to my core.

I can't help but let out a ragged gasp as he curls his finger, hitting the perfect angle that has my insides clenching around him, desperate for more. My walls pulse with need, craving the release that is on the horizon, but not close.

Thornn brushes his lips against my ear, his husky voice filling my senses. "I *own* you, Sarah," he murmurs, his possessiveness igniting an intoxicating blend of fear and desire within me. "Your body belongs to me. I'm going to make you wait, make you beg for release."

CHAPTER TWENTY

Sarah

My only other boyfriend was kind and respectful in bed. Though Thornn is kind, his forceful declarations of ownership are sending tides of sparks flooding through me. I whimper, my ass pressing back toward him, wanting to force him to take me farther, faster. Every movement, every caress, is a testament to his control, to his dominance over me. I can't deny that I crave it, that it sets me on fire.

After retreating and circling my entrance, making me whine for more, he presses the heel of his hand, teasingly grazing my throbbing bundle of nerves. Pleasure radiates outward, pooling between my thighs, and I clench my teeth to hold back a desperate moan. It's as though he knows exactly how to push me to the edge without granting me release.

The scent of desire fills the room, accompanied by the soundtrack of our heavy breaths. Sweat beads along my brow, the perspiration a tangible reminder of the heat raging within me. My skin tingles with a sensitive awareness. Every brush of his fingers is electrifying.

Thornn's touch becomes bolder, his movements deliberate as he ravishes my body, claiming it as his own. His lips graze my shoulder, then nip and suck at the sensitive flesh behind my ear, leaving a trail of sparks in their wake.

CHAPTER TWENTY

I whimper, my voice a plea for more, for the release that dances just out of reach. My fingers clench at the smooth wood of the wall, seeking an anchor in the whirlwind of sensations engulfing me.

"Patience, Sarah," Thornn whispers, his voice laced with a predatory hunger. "I'll give you what you need, but only when I decide you've earned it."

His words vibrate through me, arcing to my core. I'm at his mercy, completely surrendering to his dominance, and yet, the trust between us is growing.

His fingers continue their delicious torment, each stroke an exquisite agony that has me teetering on the edge of release. I'm on the precipice, longing to be pushed over, but Thornn knows exactly how to keep me suspended in this sweet torture.

I'm lost in a haze of desire, every nerve ending screaming for release. I writhe against his touch, aching for the ecstasy that he denies me. Thornn's cocky control is both maddening and intoxicating, pushing me to the edge while also holding me back.

But in this moment, with his possessive hands exploring every inch of my body, I trust him completely. I know that when he finally gives me what I crave, it will be beyond anything I've ever experienced.

The air is heavy with the scent of desire. My body hums with anticipation, every nerve on high alert as Thornn's possessive touch continues to ignite a primal hunger within me. The sensations swirl within me, tugging me closer to the edge.

Thornn's fingers move with purpose, brushing against my most sensitive spots, each stroke sending ripples of pleasure coursing through my veins. My skin is hypersensitive, every touch a tantalizing jolt that leaves me trembling. I can feel his tusk against my tender skin, his breath against my ear, hot and tinged with a primal hunger that matches my own.

The front of his body is molded to mine. It's only through my lusty haze that I realize he's still fully dressed, further highlighting our power differential.

His voice, deep and filled with raw desire, caresses my senses. "Beg, Sarah. Let me hear how much you want it," he murmurs, his words coaxing me further as his hand slows and provides less pressure right where I need it most. "How much you want *me*."

I can't deny him. The ache between my thighs is too potent, the need too overwhelming. I want nothing more than to feel him take me over the edge, to surrender completely to the shattering release that awaits.

My voice escapes me in a desperate plea, the words tumbling out without restraint. "Please, Thornn," I whimper, my voice laced with urgency. "I need you... make me come."

He chuckles darkly, the sound echoing through the room. Desire jolts down my spine. "Not yet, my sweet Sarah," he replies, his tone filled with a promise. "I want you wetter, dripping with need, until every fiber of your being is desperate for my touch."

His words ignite a frenzy within me, fueling the craving that pulses through my veins. I arch my back, pressing myself against his hand, silently pleading for more. My body is alive with desire, every sense heightened as the world narrows down to the electrifying connection between us.

I'm acutely aware of every sensation—his fingers exploring the curves of my body, the heat of his skin against mine, the roughness of his clothes against my back. Each touch feels like a symphony of pleasure, a tantalizing dance that drives me closer to the edge.

As his fingers continue their maddeningly slow exploration, a shudder runs through my body. It's as if every inch of me is on fire, yearning for the release that is just beyond my reach. The ache within me is deliciously unbearable, a mix of ecstasy and torment that pushes me further into the depths of my desire.

And in this intimate moment, I surrender fully to him. I trust him with my deepest, most vulnerable desires.

My breath hitches as Thornn's touch becomes bolder, his movements more deliberate. I can feel the anticipation building within me, the tension coiling tighter as each stroke brings me closer to the edge.

The symphony of pleasure crescendos, and I teeter on the precipice, on the brink of a release that promises to be earth-shattering.

As I tremble under his touch, a last plea escapes my lips, desperate and filled with longing. "Please, Thornn," I whisper, my voice pleading and needy. "I can't take it anymore. Make me come."

"Yes, my Sarah," As his feral growl reverberates through our bodies, he grants me the release I crave. "Come for me."

The world shatters around me as pleasure washes over me in a wave, crashing through me with an intensity that leaves me breathless. I arch my back, my body convulsing as the climax consumes me, obliterating everything except for the sheer ecstasy coursing through me.

I'm lost in a sea of sensation. Every touch, every stroke, every whispered word of pleasure becomes a symphony that plays out within me. Thornn's dominance, his unwavering control, guides me through this rapturous journey, taking me to heights I never thought possible.

"That's right," he whispers, then nips my shoulder tenderly, with a soft scrape of his tusks. "Good girl."

As I come down from the peak, my body still trembling with aftershocks, Thornn holds me close, his arms a safe haven.

"Such a good girl. You waited so well." His whispered praise fills a hollow place inside me I didn't know was there.

He lifts me into his arms and, as he strides through the kitchen and onto the back porch, I inspect the handsome face that has become so dear to me. Laying me down as though I'm a breakable artifact, he slides in next to me so we're facing each other.

We cup each other's cheeks at the same moment and I realize that as blissful as that experience was, it missed one thing. I couldn't look at him. Now I can get my fill as he smiles adoringly at me.

"Red? Yellow? Green?" he asks. What happened to the dominant orc that just gave me a trip to the heavens? Now he looks worried, as though he's wondering if he broke me.

"Green as grass. Green as jade. Green as my favorite orc."

He leans, not to kiss me, but to nip my bottom lip, as though the intense experience he just put me through was playacting and the real Thornn is here with me now—a mild-mannered orc who is happy to gaze into my eyes—but that's not going to continue for long.

"Your turn, big guy. You spilled your secret in the heat of passion, said you'd wanted me for days. Let me give you pleasure."

His eyes flare so wide. If I didn't know better, I'd think he was terrified.

"Nope!" He hops out of bed and is out the screen door before my eyes fully focus. "I'm going to take care of business at the stream. The games you're talking about? You're not ready for that. We'll play those games another day."

CHAPTER TWENTY-ONE

T hornn

I wake long after sunrise, my limbs tangled with Sarah's. It takes me a moment to remember what we shared last night, and another moment to believe it was real and not a dream. When my gaze travels to her face, I see her staring at me. So many emotions greet me on her gorgeous, guileless face.

Though I search for it, I see no anger, no regret. Instead, there's a tender smile playing at the corner of her lips as she gives me a questing gaze of her own. As I worry about how she's handling the brute who manhandled her and then ran away last night, it appears she's concerned about how I'm doing.

"Green as grass, green as jade, green as your favorite orc," I tell her before she even asks.

Her smile widens as she playfully slaps my biceps. "You stole my line. Make up your own."

"Okay." I pause to come up with the opposite of what she's expecting. "Green as wasabi. Green as snot. Green as Dr. Seuss's eggs."

She rewards me with a laugh, then becomes surprisingly serious.

"Have I told you how great it feels to talk to you? To hear your voice? To be treated to your thoughts? And now, to hear you joke, well, it makes me feel all warm and gooey inside."

Her expression, full of affection, takes only a moment to fill with desire.

I lean closer, breathing in her scent before I nip her bottom lip. I could get addicted to that little show of tenderness.

"First, let me apologize for running away last night. It was shitty of me. I just didn't want to press you too far, too fast."

When did I become such a liar? It wasn't to protect her tender feelings, it was to hide my secret.

"And now?" She scoots closer and tucks her leg over my thigh, a sexy, intimate act that is as subtle as a wrecking ball. To ensure I didn't miss her invitation, she adds, "I got a memo from the boss, who says we don't have to show up to work for hours." Her lewd wink adds punctuation to her brazen lie.

"Did you forget what today is? My surgery."

Her eyes fly wide with surprise. "How could I forget that? It's so important." She kisses my cheek and adds, "Don't judge. I've been distracted."

My smug look doesn't escape her.

"Okay. I'll admit, you melted my brain last night. It's a good excuse." She barely pauses before adding, "But how about now? We have a few hours."

"I do my best work after dark. Remember, I said I had a game plan. Don't worry. Besides, we've got work today. We're almost done on the main floor."

She makes another half-hearted attempt to tug my sweats off, then shrugs, rolls out of bed, and gets dressed. When we arrive in the parlor, the morning light is filtering in, illuminating dancing dust motes as Sarah and I return to work.

CHAPTER TWENTY-ONE

My muscles protest, reminding me of the countless hours of sorting and carrying, but we've made excellent progress. Only this last corner of bookshelves remains before we can pronounce the ground floor finished.

As I climb the ladder to dust off the top of the bookcase, my thoughts drift to this afternoon's surgery. I'm anxious about it, yet also hopeful. This implant represents a chance to regain some small piece of myself that was taken by those Purist monsters. My broken tusk has come to symbolize all that I lack: my voice, my confidence, my masculinity. Restoring that one fragment will help me reclaim a part of what I've lost.

I'm reminded of the aspen wood tucked in my pocket that I picked up on my walk this morning. I was itching to pull out my pocketknife and start whittling it into one of the little forest creature figurines I like to carve. Even on days when stress is high at the fire station, I find solace in the smooth, repetitive movements. Seeing the shape emerge from the untouched block of wood soothes me. Perhaps I'll have time to work on it this afternoon when I'm not supposed to do any heavy lifting.

I drag my mind back to the task at hand, grabbing armfuls of books to sort through. Most are nondescript: old classics, ancient textbooks, even some thick books on the occult. One leather-bound volume catches my eye as I add it to a stack I want to look through more thoroughly. It's a collection of fairy tales. I smile faintly, reminded of the fantastical stories some elders told about An'Wa on our feast days.

A metallic clink draws my attention as something small and green bounces across the wooden floorboards. I halt, brow furrowing. There, glittering emerald and gold against the dark wood, lies the match to the earring Sarah discovered yesterday.

My pulse leaps as I descend the ladder, then scoop it up to examine it more closely. The style matches perfectly. An oval teardrop bezel surrounded by tiny diamond accents. Strange to find it here, so far from where its mate was hidden. I call for Sarah, excitement lighting my voice.

She comes running, craning her neck to see what I've found. "The match. It was here all this time!" Her delighted grin mirrors my own as she throws her arms around me. I hug her close, breathing in the sweet floral scent of her hair.

As we embrace, laughter bubbles up past my lips. Such a small thing, this lost earring, and yet it feels monumental somehow. As if this gleaming gem represents the hidden treasure in my own life I'm just now unearthing—joy, affection, possibility. No matter what the future brings after my surgery, I vow to hold on to moments like this.

CHAPTER TWENTY-TWO

Thornn

I fidget in the hard plastic chair of Dr. Goldberg's waiting room, fingernails scraping against my blue jean clad thighs. The sterile waiting room grates on my senses—the eye-searing white walls, the harsh fluorescent lights, the antiseptic smell cloying in my nose. My stomach roils with anxiety about the impending surgery.

Sarah ran to the restroom a moment ago so she can be here before they call me back. I wish she'd return soon. Her presence soothes me. She's so relentlessly optimistic.

My ears prick at the sound of her musical laugh in the hallway outside. I'm able to tune in to the conversation, thanks to my acute orc hearing.

"Oh my gosh, Liam! I can't believe it's you!" Sarah exclaims. There's a fondness in her tone that makes my hackles rise. Who is this male?

"What are you doing here?" she continues brightly.

"It's been a while, Sarah. I got my MD, as planned. My office is down the hall."

"Wow! When we started dating in college, who knew we'd both be doctors? Although I still have a dissertation to finish. What a coincidence running into you at the dentist's office."

I sit ramrod straight as I eavesdrop on their lively conversation. Liam. Is he an old boyfriend? My gut churns and my palms sweat. I notice she didn't say she was at the dentist's office with a *friend*.

Maybe this surprise encounter will renew their relationship. My gaze falls to the floor as I remind myself that Sarah deserves someone whole, someone human. Not a miserable male of another species, one who isn't whole.

"It's so great to see you, Liam," Sarah says, warmth infusing her words.

"You look amazing," Liam returns smoothly.

There's something about the tone of his voice that makes me certain the two were intimate in the past. Physically intimate.

Was he her first? Did she love him? Does she still? I picture the two of them in the hallway, gazes locked. Perhaps he's gripping her wrist, subtly reminding her of what they once shared. In my mind's eye, he's suave, handsome, *human*. And a doctor. I'm an orc. An unemployed firefighter confined to live out his life in the Zone, behind a barbed wire fence. What have I got to offer other than a strong back, which is what she hired me for?

Icy fingers close around my heart. Of course, she would never bind herself to a broken creature like me when her accomplished, successful ex just strolled back into her life.

Their conversation continues, each lyrical laugh driving the knife deeper. I can't quit eavesdropping, no matter how much it hurts to hear them reminiscing about their past.

Liam's voice lowers in a sexy, confidential tone. "I've thought about you a lot, Sarah. Maybe we could meet up while you're still in town?" My breath strangles in my throat. "I'd love to take you out, see if that old spark is still there between us."

CHAPTER TWENTY-TWO

There's a heavy pause and I squeeze my eyes shut, awaiting her inevitable, ecstatic agreement.

"Oh, Liam..." she hedges. "I, uh..."

"Thornn." The dental assistant calls my name. I lurch to my feet, swaying with bitterness and defeat. Of course, stunning, accomplished Sarah wouldn't choose ruined, inadequate me when her accomplished ex wants her back.

I follow the assistant toward the procedure room, too miserable to even wish Sarah was beside me to hold my hand. My dream of happiness turned out to be as transient as a breeze.

CHAPTER TWENTY-THREE

S arah

It was so odd seeing Liam out in the hallway. Our senior year in college I thought he was the love of my life, but I've always been ruled by logic. My family may be wealthy, but I've never counted on being supported by anyone. That's why it was so important for me to continue my schooling, get my degree.

He got accepted into med school at the University of Colorado, and we parted ways when I went to grad school at UCLA. I consult my heart, trying to discern my true feelings. There have been many nights I've awakened from a sound sleep dreaming of him, then wondered if we might try again when we both got our degrees.

Try as I might, though, there's no spark. No pull. Just the opposite. The pull is to hurry back to the procedure room to hold my orc's hand.

My orc. Ridiculous. If either of us owns the other, he certainly owns me, at least if you believe what he said last night with his enormous hand cupped between my legs. If his actions weren't clear enough, certainly his words left nothing to the imagination.

"Where is he?" I ask the receptionist the moment I return to find his seat empty.

CHAPTER TWENTY-THREE

"I just took him back."

"Can I join him?"

"Sorry, Sarah. I thought Dr. Goldberg explained. The room is tiny. Between her and her assistant, there's no room. It won't be more than an hour." She seems almost embarrassed as she offers, "Maybe you can catch up on your Facebook?"

Sure. All I need is to doomscroll while I wait. I didn't even get to wish him good luck. As much as he tries to hide it, I know he's anxious and needs support. But rules are rules, so I pace the small waiting room, thoughts bouncing between Thornn and the surprise run-in with Liam. Of all the medical offices he could work in, what are the odds? And that he asked me out again after all this time...

My spiraling thoughts halt when the door opens and Thornn emerges, led by an assistant. He looks worse for wear with his face a paler shade of green and his muscles tense. His lower right jaw is swollen and the broken tusk has been removed. Although the end result will be a vast improvement in his self-esteem, I imagine right now he feels even worse.

I hover close as the nurse reviews post-procedure instructions. Keep the area clean, alternate cold compresses for swelling, soft diet, when to take his pain meds, take it easy for forty-eight hours. I nod along, hand drifting to rest comfortably on Thornn's arm as I commit it all to memory even though we're given a handout.

As we head to my SUV, Thornn moves slowly, clearly in pain. My heart aches for him. Back at the house, I'll make him soup and insist he rest. Knowing him, he'll fight to be back up on that ladder the moment we walk through the front door.

The drive home is quiet, tension thickening the air. I attribute it to Thornn's obvious discomfort, but can't shake the niggling sense something else is off. As I chatter about mundane topics, hoping to distract him, I realize his responses are clipped. Maybe it's the meds... or the pain... or both.

I pull up to the house, worry etching my brow. As soon as I cut the engine, Thornn is out of the car, stalking toward the woods without a backward glance. Things aren't adding up. Post-surgery pain is definitely not causing this reaction.

I hurry after him, grabbing his arm before he escapes. "Hey, what's going on?"

He fixes me with a shuttered look. "It's nothing. Forget it."

Crossing my arms, I pierce him with my most serious, almost-doctorate-in-psychology stare. "Spill it. Now."

His jaw clenches, then releases immediately as the clenching obviously hurts. His eyes are shadowed as he spews out the truth in a bitter rush. "I heard you with your ex at the dentist's office. Successful doctor Liam, who you have history with. You deserve someone like him, not a miserable beast who can't talk, can't even work. I'm half a male—broken in body and spirit. You made a mistake, slumming with me."

I gape, stunned at his conclusions. Gripping his shoulders, I force him to meet my earnest gaze. "Thornn, you couldn't be more wrong. Liam is history. He means nothing to me now. You're the one I care about."

I hold one of his big hands in mine before continuing. "As for your other concerns, you're healing, getting stronger every day. I admire you so much—your strength, courage, resilience. And I'm falling for the wonderful male you are inside."

I smile tenderly as I place my palm over his heart, tuning in for a moment to its reassuring beat. "So don't ever call yourself a miserable beast again, because to me, you're everything."

I hadn't realized how different he looks when he's angry—or hurt—until his expression softens. There's the male I'm falling for. He's so big, so strong, yet when he has that affectionate look in his eyes, it could melt the coldest heart. A warm, fuzzy feeling envelops me like a soft, protective blanket.

"I have a little surprise for you." I tug him to the front door. "You and I needed to do the junk removal and decluttering because

CHAPTER TWENTY-THREE

we don't want the hired help to throw away something valuable. But cleaning? That can be hired out. I hired Sooz's Cleaning crew, five of them, to come in while we were gone."

We climb the front porch steps and I ease through the front door, inhaling deeply. The stench of effluvia and putrefaction that once permeated this grand old house is gone, replaced by the cheerful scents of lemon and cinnamon.

I gaze around the parlor in wonder—it's barely recognizable. The dark wood floor gleams under the light streaming through the sparkling windows. Mission style tables and sideboards we've pushed out of the way after we unearthed them from under mounds of trash are now polished and shining.

My footsteps echo on the hardwood as I wander farther inside. Running my hands over the buttery soft leather couch, I can hardly believe it's real and not a hallucination. An intricate Persian rug we'd put on the wraparound porch to air has been shampooed and laid out beneath a classic mahogany mission-style rocking chair.

The wood-paneled walls have been scrubbed free of grime and lemon-oiled, which restored their rich honey tone. Filmy white curtains, having been run through the washer, now billow gently at the windows, no longer coated in layers of dirt and dust.

It seems unbelievable that this grand space could be the same hazardous dump we've been excavating for weeks. I've dreamed of the day Aunt Beth's home would be restored to its former glory. And now, gazing around this gorgeous room, I feel certain that dream is finally within reach.

"We were only gone a few hours." Thornn's voice is laced with astonishment. "Did you hire magical elves?"

It's good to hear him joke. I'm glad I allayed his fears.

"Sooz and her crew must have pulled up the moment we left and gotten to work immediately. We'll have them come back when we're done with the second floor."

When he says he's not sleepy, I pull the large mission-style rocker closer to the kitchen so we can talk while I start my not-so-world-famous pumpkin soup. It's only when he doesn't answer my question about how he feels about nutmeg, that I glance his way.

"I'm not tired, my ass," I mumble when I see his head at an almost ninety-degree angle to his body. He's out like a light.

After waking him enough to help him to the couch, I cover him with a thin blanket and watch him go back to sleep.

"You're in trouble," I whisper to myself as my heart squeezes with affection just looking at the terrifyingly handsome male as he sleeps.

I've fallen for the big guy. After all those fantasies I've had for Liam since we parted ways after senior year, I couldn't care less about his request for a date. Instead, I'm sweet on Thornn.

As I return to the kitchen to finish chopping the onion, a feeling of unease settles over me when I think about how, exactly, I'm going to mention to my parents that the guy I'm falling for is an orc who lives in the Integration Zone. I can hear their responses now, and, at least in my imagination, that conversation is not going to be pretty.

CHAPTER TWENTY-FOUR

Thornn

I wake feeling refreshed, the ache in my jaw much improved from yesterday's surgery. One benefit of being an orc—we heal swiftly. I wiggle my jaw slowly, testing my sore muscles. Finding the pain manageable, I rise from the couch where Sarah tucked me in yesterday after I conked out.

My senses awaken to delicious scents wafting from the kitchen. I follow my nose and find Sarah at the stove, wooden spoon in hand as she stirs a pot emitting mouthwatering aromas of onions, garlic, and spices.

She turns, greeting me with a radiant smile. "Good morning! I figured soup would go easy on your jaw for lunch later today. Scrambled eggs will be coming right up. I was just waiting for you to wake up, sleepyhead. How are you feeling?"

"Much better, thanks to your TLC... and my orc constitution. We heal faster than humans." I smile back, warmed by her thoughtfulness and the cozy domesticity of this scene.

I was born in the Zone to a mother who mated the first male who showed an interest in her. Some orcs are lucky enough to find their soulbound mates. They see each other in a red haze and bond for life with a deep soul connection. My parents weren't so lucky. Their mating was one of convenience, not affection.

They both loved me. My chest squeezes in sadness as I relive the anguish I felt when they died last year. Our tenement ceiling collapsed on them when I was out on a fire call. I miss them every day. Although they expressed affection to me, they didn't show much of it to each other. I rarely observed scenes of quiet connectedness like the one I'm experiencing right now.

I don't have to fight to get a word in as I used to do as I shared meals with the other orcs in the firehouse. I don't have to fill our quiet moments with unnecessary words. Sarah accepts my thoughts and is eager to hear my opinions. Being with Sarah is comfortable... easy.

Well, not all our moments are easy. There was nothing easy when I pressed her up against the wall and edged her higher until she was panting, begging for release. I shake those thoughts out of my mind when, a short while later over plates of cheesy eggs, we make plans to tackle the second floor.

"You sure you're up for it? Your jaw is still swollen, and you slept for sixteen hours."

"Exactly. I slept for sixteen hours." Rubbing my jaw gingerly with my palm, I reassure myself that I'm not in too much pain. "I'm a little sore, but work won't bother me."

She points her fork at me, swallows her bite, and orders, "You just tell me if it starts to throb or ache and we'll quit for the day. You can take a nap while I sort through all those white bags waiting for me on the front porch. I still can't fathom why Beth saved magazines and newspapers like that."

"I googled it. It's a mental condition. Often the people know their behavior isn't right. That's why they call it a compulsion. They can't help it."

She spears me with an appreciative look. "That's really thoughtful of you, Thornn, trying to understand her. I've been trying not to get angry at her for letting things get to this point, but you're right. She couldn't help it."

A couple of days ago, I navigated through the goat paths on the wide, wooden steps to the second floor and took a quick peek

CHAPTER TWENTY-FOUR

around. Just thinking about mucking out all those neglected rooms and corridors makes me weary, but the sooner we complete this task, the sooner I can sort through my conflicted feelings and make a decision about my future... and my heart.

We trudge up the grand staircase, which I cleared before my surgery, and I groan at the sight. Heaps of clothing, books, boxes, and unidentifiable rubbish greet us, coating every surface. At least it lacks the hellish stench of downstairs. Small favors.

Sarah surveys the mess dubiously. "Where should we start?"

I point toward an ornate doorway. "The master suite?"

"It's as good a place as any. If I were to hide my treasures, I imagine the good stuff would be close to me."

I follow her inside and we get to work. After hours of sorting and hauling loads downstairs, we've made a sizable dent in the clutter.

Sarah wipes her brow, grinning. "When I was a teen hiding things from my parents, I used to hide stuff under my dresser drawers, taped to the bottom. Maybe the sneaky part of my aunt's brain was a lot like mine."

I almost let that statement slide by without comment, but I can't refrain from asking, "Tell me, Sarah. What did a *good girl* like you hide?"

It's clear she loves to be praised when her arousal scent spikes, waking up my dormant cock. The scent has been swirling around her for days, but it was camouflaged by the house's stench. I much prefer this aroma.

"I'm not sure I should share how naughty I was as a teen." Her blue eyes sparkle with mischief. "In high school, I got pretty good at hiding joints from my parents."

"Never got caught?" My eyebrow wings up in question.

"Nope."

I think of all the fun ways I'd like to punish her, but push that aside when she gets back to work.

Kneeling, she slides out the bottom drawer of an imposing bird's-eye maple antique dresser. I join her on the floor, pulse quickening. If Aunt Beth secreted things away like teenage Sarah did, what might we uncover in these old bureaus?

Sarah gasps, withdrawing a faded manila envelope. With quivering fingers, she shakes out an official-looking document. "A bearer bond!"

I whoop with excitement. In minutes, the two of us are yanking out dresser drawers and turning them over to inspect the undersides.

"Here's another! We struck the mother lode!" Sarah crows in the most adorable, unladylike manner. Her exhilaration thrills me. It makes her blue eyes dance.

An hour later, the area is strewn with upended drawers and growing piles of envelopes and documents. Sarah keeps up a delighted narrative about her windfall.

"Mmm, Montgomery Ward. They went out of business in the last millennium," she says with a smirk. "I imagine this one's worthless, though I'll check it out."

I hand her another promising slip of paper. "How about this?"

"Woot! IBM. I can't imagine what that one's worth. And look!" She holds up another with very impressive curly-Qs adorning all four sides. "Proctor and Gamble! I'll have to send my parents a text. If they ever connect to Wi-Fi, they're going to get a big surprise." She reaches for another manilla envelope, a wide smile on her face.

Watching Sarah unwrap each new discovery fills me with excitement and tenderness. However complicated my situation, I know one truth deep in my soul—somehow, I need to find a way to remain by her side. If she'll have me.

CHAPTER TWENTY-FIVE

Sarah

I sit back on my heels, stunned at the small fortune in bearer bonds and antique stocks we've uncovered over the past few hours. My fingertips tingle from where I gripped each slip of paper, my heart racing with exhilaration over this unexpected windfall.

I can hardly wrap my mind around the implications. Unlike some of my privileged classmates who enjoyed lavish allowances, I've always worked hard for everything I have. My parents never spoiled me, wanting me to appreciate the value of money. Thanks to Aunt Beth's secretive hoarding, I now have wealth of my own.

I try to quell the surge of giddiness, not wanting to lose focus on the monumental task still ahead—restoring order to this grand old house. We may have cleared the lower level of hazardous clutter, but the upstairs remains a disaster zone. I force my attention back to the job, grabbing another armload of clothing to sort and pack for donation.

As I smooth out one of my aunt's summery dresses, my thoughts inevitably circle back to the sexy male across from me. Thornn meets my gaze, one brow quirked, a question in his tawny eyes. Even disheveled from hours of labor, he takes my breath away.

Will coming into money complicate things between us? Now that I have means of my own, will he feel there's too much of a gap between us? I ache to prove to Thornn that my feelings are sincere. I've gotten to know this male well, spending every waking and sleeping moment with him for the past few weeks. His inner beauty moves me as much as his outer magnificence.

I want to show him tenderness and patience until he trusts me enough to confide his secrets. My instincts tell me painful wounds lurk beneath that stoic armor. When he's ready, I'll prove he can rely on me. For now, I vow to chip away, little by little, at the barricades around his heart.

I meet his gaze again, flashing a playful smile. "Maybe we should celebrate our progress tonight. We threw away all the food, but I kept Beth's stash of wine." I wink.

His answering grin stirs butterflies low in my belly. Perhaps, if the mood is right, we might revisit the passion we shared when he pressed me against the wooden panel and touched me as though he *owned* me. I shiver, recalling his dominant intensity, how his possessive touch ignited such powerful pleasure. If he wants to claim me tonight, I'll surrender completely.

As I work in one closet, Thornn sorts through a cluttered closet on the other side of the room. He pulls out a handful of men's dress shirts and slacks. The outdated styles and faded fabric hint they've been here for decades.

"These must have belonged to your Aunt Beth's husband. What was his name again?"

"Fred," I reply, a wave of sadness washing over me. "He died when I was really young. I don't remember him, though Beth showed me pictures of me on his lap. He had an affectionate smile on his face when he gazed at me."

Thornn nods thoughtfully. "Losing a mate must have devastated her. Do you think that could have triggered her hoarding?"

"I wouldn't be surprised." I picture Aunt Beth, alone and grieving, unable to part with Fred's possessions. My heart aches for her suffering.

CHAPTER TWENTY-FIVE

As we talk, Thornn unearths a collection of garish vintage neckties. He holds one up, the shiny orange and green paisley pattern almost luminous.

I chuckle. "Groovy ties. Very 1970s."

Thornn gives me a sly sideways glance, one corner of his mouth curling upward. He loops the tie around his hand, snapping it taut.

"I can think of some creative new uses for these ties," he says, his deep voice dipping an octave.

My belly flutters at the blatant promise in his heated gaze. I lean closer, swatting his rock-hard biceps. I don't want to make him uncomfortable by mentioning how sexy he looks with only one tusk—dangerous, piratical.

"Behave yourself," I scold playfully. But inside, I'm thrilled at this glimpse of his flirtatious side. Later, when I'm bound helpless by those gaudy ties, I imagine the tables will be turned as to who is scolding whom.

CHAPTER TWENTY-SIX

Thornn

We worked until after sundown last night, which seemed like poor timing for the kind of bedroom activities I had in mind. Besides, my mouth was still tender, which would definitely cramp my style. Using all my self-control, I didn't pursue the flirtation we shared all day, silently vowing to make good on my lusty cravings today.

I'm going to ensure we knock off at five this afternoon. Before then, though, I do a load of laundry, and make sure the master bedroom is perfectly clean with fresh linens. I have plans.

Sarah must sense my intentions, because whenever I glance her way, she's already looking at me, an interested expression on her face. We're both working at breakneck speed to get this room decluttered, swept, and dusted. Great minds think alike.

When the bedroom is spick and span, I announce, "Let's have a light dinner. I don't want either of us to be too full for tonight's entertainment." Although I don't think I've ever done it before, I discover I can waggle my eyebrows.

I must have managed to do it without looking ridiculous, because a lusty smile slashes across Sarah's pretty face as she says, "Yes, sir," then adds a snappy salute.

CHAPTER TWENTY-SIX 103

"Although I don't know about the salute, I'd like you to keep the yes, sirs for later." I'm not sure whether it's the lewd pictures flicking through my mind that cause my cock to thicken under my pants, or the soft, breathless gasp that escapes her lips.

I decide to make us a simple salad with grilled chicken for dinner. My father taught me how to cook. He explained that it's a male's duty and privilege to cook for his mate. It's part of the courting ritual. He loved to cook for mom and me. Even if it was out of obligation, not affection, he did it with pride.

While I chop the vegetables, I catch glimpses of Sarah out of the corner of my eye, her nimble hands whisking the homemade dressing with a seductive grace. The scent of the fresh basil and tangy balsamic vinegar fills the kitchen, mixing with the anticipation that hangs heavy between us.

I feel a sense of pride as I cook for her. Focusing on that helps me push my arousal to the recesses of my mind. I've never cooked for a female I was courting, never felt so close to anyone before. I've heard the phrase "we clicked," but it never really made sense until this moment.

Sarah and I work wordlessly without having to divide the chores. Everything just comes naturally. And she's always happy. Well, that's not true. The woman was far from happy when I had her up against the wall the other day. She was so intense, so aroused...

Forcing myself back into the moment, I plate the food and we sit down at the dining table in the formal dining room, which is now clean, the honey oak furniture gleaming.

The flicker of candlelight dances in Sarah's sky-blue eyes. As the warm aroma of the food fills the air around us, she takes a bite of the salad, her lips parting slightly in pleasure. The way she savors the flavors, the culinary adventure on her taste buds, makes my mind fast forward to the joys that await us upstairs.

"This is delicious," she murmurs as she takes a sip of what she informed me was one of Beth's better bottles of wine. I feel a surge of pride knowing I've brought her pleasure not only in the kitchen but soon, in the bedroom as well.

I smile, my voice low and husky as I reply, "I'm glad you enjoy it. But I have a feeling the real feast has yet to come." The double entendre hangs heavy in the air, and her cheeks flush a delicate shade of pink.

After we finish our meal, we clear the table in silence. When the counters are wiped clean, our eyes meet, her expression full of anticipation and promise. I grip her hand, and the tension thickens around us as we make our way to the master bedroom.

My heart pounds, my palms growing clammy with nervous excitement. My anticipation surges when I see the array of colorful ties I left in neat rows on top of what Sarah calls the lowboy dresser. I made no secret as I took my time laying them out before we went down to dinner. I wanted Sarah to be filled with expectation as much as I was.

"Stand at the foot of the bed." My voice is deep, filled with command. After our encounter in the parlor, with her naked against the paneled wall, she knows what she's getting into. I don't need to ease her into this. If she can't handle me as I am, it's best for all concerned to discover that now.

She immediately follows my direction.

"Take off your clothes."

I step backward until my back touches the wall across from her and silently watch. Although she was stark naked when she approached me in the parlor, now that I'm in charge, she seems skittish as a doe in the forest. Although her fingers are trembling, she removes her t-shirt.

Am I being too harsh? Going too fast? She's human, soft, and feminine. Perhaps I'm terrifying her. "Green, yellow, or red, Sarah?"

"Green. It's just nerves, Sir."

Holy fuck. She said Sir and my cock, already rock-hard, somehow stiffened in my pants. If she keeps calling me that, I'm going to come before I even touch her.

CHAPTER TWENTY-SIX

"Remove the rest of your clothes, fold them, and put them on the lowboy, near the ties."

She slowly, sensuously, takes off each piece of clothing. Her nipples harden as I watch. Now that the terrible stink is gone, I can smell Sarah's arousal scent most of the day. It reminds me of cloves, heady and tingly on the tongue. Usually, it simmers in the background, but now it's flared, powerful enough that another orc might smell it from blocks away. Good thing there aren't any other orcs within a thousand miles.

"You saw the ties. Anything I could do with them that you might object to?"

"No, Sir."

If our relationship continues, perhaps someday that word will lose its power over me. In the meantime, I focus on how much this woman trusts me. It makes me feel even more affection for her, my chest warm and tight.

I grab one of the thick ties from the 70s, bring it to her eyes, and tie it tightly behind her head.

"Too tight?"

She shakes her head.

"Speak."

"No, Sir."

With one hand on each of her shoulders, I dance her backward until her thighs hit the mattress, then help her to the middle of the clean, soft quilt.

Her breath is heaving. I imagine it's partly from arousal and partly from fear. I'm doing it on purpose, making certain her attention is one hundred percent focused on my instructions... and her arousal.

"Lie down."

She complies quickly, her arousal scent still strong, although her fear scent curls lightly through the room.

"Reach up and grab the bedposts." After she complies, I carefully loop and tie her wrists to the headboard. Her breath quickens, her chest rising and falling with anticipation.

With her blindfolded, I have no reservations about removing my clothes. I'm fully in charge. Her eyes are sightless. Her hands can't reach between my legs. My shameful secret is safe.

I take my time, savoring every inch of her body with my hands, my lips, my tongue.

Moving down her body, I start at her neck, nipping and sucking. At first, I'm gentle, but it's when I suck too hard and leave a mark that she pants with arousal.

"You like it rough, Sarah." It's a statement, not a question. I don't want her to have to think, to speak. "I just want you to feel."

Continuing, I leave marks that will remind her of my dominance long after this night is over. Her skin is warm and soft against my rough, calloused hands, a perfect contrast that fuels my desire. I move lower, tracing circles with my tongue around her sensitive nipples, then stabbing and flicking them, as she arches into my touch.

I play with one nipple while I suckle on the other. At first, I'm tender, using the soft pads of my fingertips. When I pluck, her head thrashes on the pillow, and when I tug harder, she sucks air in with a pleasured gasp.

Exploring what brings her bliss, I learn her limits, stopping the moment I cross the boundary of pleasure into pain.

When I first told her to lie down, her thighs seemed superglued together, but the more I arouse her, the louder her gasps and moans become, and the farther apart she spreads her thighs.

I reach to cup her there, having already learned how to touch her to heighten her awareness and arousal without giving her an ounce of pleasure. My palm is wet from her cream. I imagine it

CHAPTER TWENTY-SIX 107

wouldn't be hard to push her over the edge, but that's not going to happen for a while.

Her plaintive, wordless whines fill the room, encouraging me to continue my exploration. I trail kisses and nibbles down her abdomen, reveling in the way her muscles tense beneath my touch. Sliding my tongue along the seam of her thighs, I tease her, never quite reaching the core of her desire.

Her hips buck, silently begging for more, but I keep my own desires in check, savoring the salty taste of her skin as I inch closer to her heat. Finally, I give in to her silent plea, stretching her thighs wide, parting her folds with my tongue, and delving my black tongue deep into her wetness.

Her moans reach a crescendo, growing louder and more desperate with each plunge of my tongue, each flick against her sensitive clit. I relish the taste of her, the way she clenches around me, and I can feel my own need building with each passing moment.

Pulling away, I hear her whimper of frustration, but I have so much more in store for her.

"Color?"

"Jade, Sir. The color of your skin."

"Mmm." For that, I reach up to nuzzle her neck, nipping one of her tendons in appreciation.

Because I left my post between her legs, I allow her passion to cool a bit by slowly making my way down her body again, licking, nipping, and breathing hot gusts of air across her already fevered skin.

She arches her back, straining against her bindings, but there is no escape from my control. I watch intently as she writhes beneath me, knowing that I hold her pleasure in my hands.

"I'm going to make you come on my tongue, Sarah. Want that?"

"Yes, please."

I nip her mound, then thrust my tongue so deeply into her wet heat that it pulls a shocked gasp from her. Orc tongues are longer than humans', so I find her magic spot on the front wall of her channel while I press tight circles against her clit with the pad of my finger.

I've never been with a human female but from what I've read and seen on the internet they are built the same as orc females, only more delicate. I'm happy to discover that's true.

I guess I'd ramped her up with the binding and the foreplay, because she explodes into her orgasm with a wordless shout. Her thighs tighten against my cheeks as I work her through her release, tongue-fucking her with wild thrusts.

Her cries fill the air as she tumbles into ecstasy, her body pulsing around me. I continue delving into her, rhythmically riding out her pleasure, prolonging it with fingers and tongue.

"Thornn!" My name is a cry, a plea, at once both a thank you and a request for more.

I'm hard and leaking pre-cum. For a moment, I consider untying her, then plunging into her, but I'm not ready for her to discover my secret. It would ruin everything.

The idea of pistoning into her with her wrists bound leaves a foul taste in my mouth. Dominance games are fun. They're part and parcel of who I am, but they're not meant for our first time together. That needs to be full of affection, not command.

I pull my thin sweats back on, then collapse beside her. Using all the energy swirling inside me, coiled for release, I redirect it into a hundred kisses on her cheeks and jaw and throat. The room is filled with heavy breathing and the scent of sex as I slowly remove her blindfold and untie her wrists, taking care not to mar her delicate skin.

She rolls on top of me and presses both hands to my cheeks as she holds my gaze in hers.

"That was amazing. You made me boneless. You're... gifted. Now, let me make you feel just as good."

CHAPTER TWENTY-SIX 109

She moves so quickly I almost don't stop her in time as she tries to slide her hand beneath my waistband. Gripping her wrist, I shake my head no.

"You might not be ready for an orc cock, little Sarah. For that, you'll have to wait."

I'm such a fucker. I just hinted that this is about her inadequacy, not mine. If we ever get to the point where I can divulge my secret, I hope she'll understand. I'm surprised when, instead of arguing, she gives me a naughty smile, tosses her long, brown hair, and straddles me so her slit is riding the hard ridge of my cock through my soft pants.

"There's more than one way to get you off."

With that, she begins to ride me and, Goddess help me, I don't order her to stop.

Although she just came with the force of a neutron bomb, Sarah's desire is evident in the way her body moves against mine. The scent of her arousal fills the air, intertwining with the lingering fragrance of our earlier passion. Pressing her palms to my pecs, her eyes shutter in pleasure.

The sight of her above me is intoxicating. Her skin flushes with pleasure, her breasts rise and fall with each breath, and her hair cascades over her shoulders, a wild and enticing tangle. I grip her hips, relishing the softness beneath my calloused palms. Her eyes, filled with desire and trust, lock onto mine, and I feel a surge of emotion overwhelm me.

As Sarah moves, I close my eyes and focus on the sensations. The rhythm of her hips as she rides me, the press of her private parts against mine, separated only by a thin layer of fabric.

I listen to the symphony of our breaths mingling, the sounds of her moans and sighs filling the room. I didn't think either of us could come like this, but not only is she driving my arousal higher with every grinding slide, but her breathing is coming faster, as though she's approaching another release of her own.

It's a chorus of ecstasy, a melody of our desires intertwining. The way she moves, the way she gasps my name, fuel the fire within me, making me ache for release.

I hook a hand on her nape and pull her close to capture her lips with mine, tasting the salt on her skin. The kiss is fierce and hungry, a collision of passion and need. Our tongues dance together, exploring, tasting, and seeking solace in the depth of our connection. The taste of her on my lips is addictive, and I can't get enough.

I run my hands over her body, tracing the contours of her curves, feeling the heat radiating from her. Every touch is deliberate, a testament to my desire for her. I revel in the texture of her skin beneath my fingertips, the softness and warmth that contrasts with the roughness of my orcish nature.

The primal scent of our lovemaking, a heady mix of sweat, musk, and desire hangs in the air. It ignites something primal within me, fueling my need to possess and claim her as mine. Inhaling deeply, I let it fill my senses, intensifying the connection between us.

As Sarah's movements grow more urgent, the tension builds within me, the need for release growing stronger with each passing second. I grip her hips, guiding her with gentle nudges, meeting her movements with my own, surrendering to the sea of sensations that envelop us both.

As she reaches her own climax, I allow myself to join her. It's an explosion of pleasure that rips through me, threatening to tear down the walls I've built to hide my secrets. I grunt my pleasure, letting her know what she does to me, then remember I've found my tongue. I can speak to her with words.

"Sarah," I breathe when she collapses onto me. "I don't deserve you." She doesn't want to hear my latest mantra, which is that she deserves so much better than me. Instead, I kiss her, smooth her hair back, and speak some of the few orcish words I know.

"*Lach lamon khondragon. Tramon dirmen bonvaggo,* Sarah."

"Mmm," her voice is low, a sleepy look on her beautiful face.

CHAPTER TWENTY-SIX

It's obvious. Our connection goes beyond the physical, beyond dominance and submission. It's a bond that transcends our differences, bringing us together in a dance of passion and understanding.

And as we lay there, entwined in each other's arms, our bodies still humming with the aftershocks of pleasure, I can't help but feel a glimmer of hope.

I thought she was asleep, but when I purr for her the first time, her heavy lids flutter open and gaze at me in surprised wonder.

"You're purring?"

"A bit of orc magic to calm my—" I stop myself before I say the word mate, which would probably make the tired woman in my arms run for the hills. "To calm you and express my affection."

"Can you do it forever?" Her voice is dreamy, faraway. "You're right. It's magical."

CHAPTER TWENTY-SEVEN

Sarah

I wake slowly, blinking against the early morning light filtering into our bedroom. Our bedroom. The thought brings a smile to my lips. After weeks of living and working side-by-side, this grand old mansion feels like home, and Thornn feels like family.

I stretch lazily, reaching across the rumpled sheets, seeking Thornn's warmth. Finding his side of the bed empty, I sit up, the flannel nightgown I wore to bed slipping off one shoulder. Where is he?

Since discovering the hidden gems and bearer bonds, we've worked with feverish intensity to meet the inspection deadline. We pushed ourselves to the brink of exhaustion day after day, sorting through endless piles of clutter. Thankfully, we got another visit from Sooz and her crew yesterday to dust and make everything, upstairs and down, sparkle.

Just yesterday, Thornn spent hours removing junk from a dilapidated shed at the back of the sprawling property. When he returned hours later, grinning triumphantly, my brows rose in question.

Wordlessly, he held out his green palm, revealing three exquisite antique cocktail rings—a ruby, an emerald, and a sapphire, each set in intricate gold filigree and surrounded by sparkling

CHAPTER TWENTY-SEVEN

diamonds. He explained how he found them tucked in a jar filled with screws and hardware buried deep on a cluttered shelf. If not for his sharp eyes, I might have lost the rings to the landfill. I'm glad he found those because my tireless excavation of the white bags of yellowed magazines and newspapers netted nothing of worth.

Waking alone after so many mornings tangled together feels odd. I grab a cup of coffee from the carafe he made and find Thornn in the backyard on the old-fashioned metal glider we unearthed as he stares pensively out at the sweeping mountain vista.

"Your coffee's perfect this morning, as usual," I murmur, savoring the dark roast that I loaded with plenty of cream as I sit in the glider next to him. "You're up early."

He drapes an arm around my shoulders, and I lean into him with a contented sigh. We watch the sunrise over the mist rising from the stream. So much has changed in a few short weeks. The house, the fortune we discovered, and most of all, us. We've forged a profound connection I never expected, but am so lucky to have found.

My pulse trips faster as I realize what today represents. If everything goes well, it will be our last day here before returning to L.A., to real life. What will that mean for us? I have no idea, but I know what I *want*. This male isn't just for today, but for all my tomorrows. I want to prove that what we've built here can thrive beyond the calm safety of this mountain home.

I tip my head back, seeking Thornn's amber gaze. Though I've never uttered the L word, he deserves to know how I feel before decisions are made, before we leave.

"Thornn, I..." My confession dies on my lips as a vehicle rumbles up the gravel drive.

Thornn stiffens. "The inspector is early! I'll go to the stream to hide."

"You'll do no such thing!" He tries to interrupt me, but I'm having none of it. "Orcs may not be a common sight here in Colorado, but they're legal. You have every right to leave the Zone, every right to be here with me."

"*I* know that and *you* know that, but *they* might not. And, face it, even if they do, if they're prejudiced against me, they will take it out on you. It's no big deal for me to hide while they're here. This inspection is too important for it to fail because of me."

Anger flies through me that this wonderful male feels the need to lurk in the shadows to protect me. Then affection takes my fury's place as I realize he's willing to put his desire to help me above his own pride.

When I recall his abject fear at McDonald's and at the rest stop that first day, I wonder if he'd rather not be around human strangers, so I soften. "If you *want* to stay away, be my guest, Thornn. But if you want to stay, I'd be *proud* to have you at my side because you always have my back."

Time is of the essence. The inspector might be standing on my doorstep by now, but I give Thornn time to think.

"It will give you comfort if I'm with you?" His head is tipped to the side in disbelief, as though the concept of me wanting him nearby makes no sense.

"Absolutely."

"Then let's get a move on."

He grips my hand, and together we round the corner of the house as two men step out of a small blue government sedan. They're both wearing blue polos and khaki pants, along with stern expressions.

"Good morning!" I call out with forced cheerfulness as I walk to meet them. Thornn is a solid, reassuring presence beside me.

The inspectors eye Thornn warily. One is tall and reedy, with gray hair cropped close to his skull. The other is shorter and barrel-chested, with a bristling salt-and-pepper mustache.

CHAPTER TWENTY-SEVEN 115

"I'm Sarah, the owner. Thank you for coming to reinspect the property. This is my... This is Thornn "

The mustached man steps forward, clipboard in hand. "I'm Stan Hubble, county building inspector. This is my partner, Bill Stiles. We're here to determine if this property still poses health and safety risks requiring condemnation."

I eye the two inspectors warily. My heart pounds, nerves jangling despite my confident words to Thornn. So much hangs on this inspection going well. I lead them to the house and climb the steps.

"Please, come inside." Stomach knotted with nerves, I usher them toward the imposing carved oak doors.

Their boots thump heavily on the gleaming wood floors as we enter the spacious foyer. I hold my breath, praying they won't notice the cobweb I only now see hanging from the antler chandelier in the middle of the ceiling.

Stan's mustache twitches as his shrewd gaze sweeps the area. I wince as he scribbles on his clipboard. Thornn tenses beside me, arms folded across his broad chest in an attempt to look casual.

We continue into the parlor. Stan pokes behind furniture with his metal clipboard while Bill runs a finger across the mantle.

"Looks clean enough," Bill mutters. My shoulders ease down an inch.

"Hmph." Stan's noncommittal grunt spikes my anxiety again.

As we tour each room, the inspection seems to drag on endlessly. Stan continues scribbling notes, face impassive. Thornn trails the three of us silently, tension radiating from him in waves.

The questions start in the kitchen. Stan raps his knuckles against appliances. "All in working order?" Before I can respond, his beady eyes turn to Thornn. "I suppose you did the manual labor while the little lady stayed clean?"

Thornn's jaw tightens, but he remains silent. I step forward, irked. "We worked side by side. Thornn was invaluable." Stan smirks and makes a humph noise in the back of his throat before moving on.

Upstairs, Bill sticks an electrical gizmo into outlets. He addresses me while blatantly staring at Thornn. "He give you any trouble? I hear they can get pretty aggressive."

Heat flushes my cheeks. Calling him *they*? Talking about him as though he's not here although he's not ten feet away?

I meet Bill's gaze coolly. "None whatsoever. Thornn is a gentleman."

Bill and Stan snort in unison and their gazes meet over my head. I can't imagine the conversation they're going to have on their way home. On second thought, I *can* imagine it. I'll bet good money they discuss the possibility that Thornn and I have been sharing the master bedroom although we made sure to leave no evidence of that.

After a thorough inspection of every closet and cabinet, we finish in the master suite. Stan gives a curt nod.
After sharing a whispered conversation with Bill, he says, "Vast improvement. No longer hazardous. You'll get a letter confirming you've remediated the problems noted in our original correspondence." He turns to Thornn with a scowl. "See that you continue to behave. We wouldn't want any incidents."

I don't risk even a glance at Thornn, not wanting to see what I imagine will be anger and humiliation on his face. Even though I'm not looking at him, I can sense every muscle in his body tighten. I need to keep my cool until these jerks leave. After they pull out of the driveway, there will be plenty of time to dissect every shitty thing these men said and did.

With a long exhale, I walk them out, anxiety draining every step closer to the door we get. Thornn stands tall and silent at my side, but I sense his discomfort. We wait, motionless, as they get into their car and pull forward into the circular drive.

CHAPTER TWENTY-SEVEN

When they're finally out of sight, I crow, "We did it!" Without the two men's condescending attitude, I'd be whooping, hollering, and considering opening one of Aunt Beth's better bottles of wine in celebration. Instead, I hurtle into Thornn's arms, pressing my cheek against his expansive chest.

"I wanted to hurt those fuckers," I admit.

"Yeah, but violence doesn't solve anything."

My eyes grow wide when I realize who I'm talking to. This is the guy who lost a tusk and got scars and broken bones when Purists battered him. If anyone should be irate, it should be Thornn.

I've been thinking about the future a lot since Thornn and I have grown intimate. Most of my daydreams involved us making things permanent here in this mansion, but I doubt he'll ever feel comfortable outside the Zone. I understand his feelings more every time something like this happens.

CHAPTER TWENTY-EIGHT

Thornn

As I gently set another box down amidst the other containers and suitcases in the back of the Subaru, a pang of unease shoots through me. It's hard to believe our time at the mansion is ending. Over the past weeks, this place has gone from being torturous to becoming a sanctuary for Sarah and me.

We've forged a bond through long days of labor and passionate nights of intimacy. She still doesn't know my secret, and certainly must wonder why I've never gotten naked with her, much less thrust into her wet, willing heat but she's respected me enough not to press the issue and ask directly. I'll have to trust her with the hard facts soon, or my lack of intimacy will destroy our relationship.

Two days ago, I returned to the dentist for a quick check of the site where she implanted the screw. Dr. Goldberg was impressed with how well the extraction site had healed. I had one dose of painkillers following the procedure and haven't needed any since then.

I can't wait for the new tusk to be inserted. The broken tusk was demoralizing, but having only one is so much worse. I don't think about it much when I'm alone with Sarah because it doesn't seem to make any difference to her. The thought of facing all the Others in the Zone has my anxiety spiking.

CHAPTER TWENTY-EIGHT 119

As we load the last of our belongings, I take a final look around the yard I've come to know so well—the shed where I unearthed Sarah's antique rings, the path to the stream where I bathed under starry skies.

So much has changed since I've been here. I found my voice, a piece of myself I thought was lost forever. And somehow, miraculously, I won the heart of an incredible woman along the way. Neither of us has uttered the L word, but I'm sure of my feelings and have a hunch Sarah reciprocates them.

She silently joins me, slipping her soft hand in mine. Her wistful smile tells me her thoughts mirror my own. Without a word, we turn back to the SUV, our movements in sync. Over weeks together, we've learned each other's rhythms—when to step in to lend a hand and when to give space.

"I heard from my parents yesterday," Sarah says brightly as she tapes up the last box. "They finally got my messages when they docked in Rome. Of course, I left out certain details." She winks playfully. "But they're thrilled I salvaged Aunt Beth's house... and that I'm not traveling home alone."

Her words make my heart squeeze. I've avoided thinking about what happens next. About me, an orc from the Integration Zone, returning to the real world. And about navigating a relationship some will never understand. I'm starting to question if I was mistaken to think she feels the same way about me, given that she hasn't revealed our relationship to her parents. Why hasn't she mentioned me to them? Then I calm my nerves, reminding myself that although we've spent every waking and sleeping hour together, we've only known each other a month.

Sarah seems to read my thoughts. She cups my cheek, her sky-blue eyes earnest. "I care about you, Thornn." Her thumb caresses my skin. "All the problems that face us? We'll figure them out together."

I cover her slender hand with mine and lift her palm to my lips for a tender kiss, then pull her close. We cling together for a long moment before stepping apart to finish loading the car.

Soon we're barreling down the winding mountain road away from the mansion, toward the unknown future. But with Sarah's hand tucked safely in mine, I've never felt more optimistic about what lies ahead.

CHAPTER TWENTY-NINE

Sarah

Although so much has changed since our journey to Colorado a month ago, it's as though I can see Thornn regressing in front of my eyes. We weren't five miles from the mansion before he asked me to pull over.

He exited, rummaged in his duffel, and returned to the front seat wearing that green hoodie from the day I met him. And it wasn't because he's cold. I know that because the interior of the car is plenty warm enough, especially for him. Besides, he certainly doesn't need to wear his hood over his head while we're indoors.

I'm so tuned in to him now I can practically feel his muscles tightening under that beautiful jade skin. At the Verdant Park McDonald's drive-through, he hunched down, facing the passenger window so he couldn't be seen.

When we stop in Denver for a coffee refill, though he says nothing, his urge for me to hurry is clear in the plaintive look in his eyes. I half expect him to start texting me instead of talking.

Although I try to stop as infrequently as possible, determined to settle for the snacks and drinks we brought, the car can't go without a fill-up. Pulling off into a small town, I decide to gamble on gas station coffee as I fill up the car. For Thornn, gas stations are the worst part of the trip because there's nowhere to hide.

Between the cashier having to refill the coffee pot and the bathroom being a one-seater and having three people in line, it's a hot minute before I return to the car.

"Shit!"

Four young men, in their teens or early twenties, are rocking my white Forester—with Thornn in it.

I drop my coffee in my haste as I launch toward them, all the while screaming, "Stop that, you fuckers!"

One of them has a one-by-two board spiked with nails that he either brought to the party or found in the dumpster.

"Somebody call 911!" I shout as, adrenaline pumping, I sprint toward the car, leaving my spilled coffee splattered on the cracked blacktop. The four thugs are violently rocking the SUV as they spit vulgar curses.

"Animal!"

"Monster!"

"Fuck freaks!"

"Go back to where you came from!"

The back of my mind imagines Thornn would like nothing better than to magically transport back to An'Wa. Heart pounding, my fingers tremble as I reach for my phone to dial 911 since I don't think anyone in the parking lot has done so.

"Stop! Stop that, you assholes!" I scream, my voice cracking with desperation. "I'm calling the police."

One of the attackers, the one wielding the spiked board, turns toward me with a malicious grin.

Although I'm not safe out here, I scream to Thornn, "DON'T GET OUT!"

These guys may be fuckers, but I doubt it's me they want to hurt. The moment Thornn leaves the car, they'll attack him, and

CHAPTER TWENTY-NINE

by the look of things, they'll show no mercy. Hasn't he been through enough?

Thornn's face is like a thundercloud of anger. When I lock eyes with him through the bug-splattered windshield, I shake my head vehemently, the look on my face begging him to stay put. I couldn't bear to see the male I'm falling in love with being attacked by these animals.

Without thinking, I charge the nearest attacker, aiming to disrupt their assault on the car. The spiked board swings through the air, narrowly missing me as I dodge to the side. Panic surges through me as I realize I'm not immune to their hate.

"Back off! Just back the hell off!" I shout, trying to assert authority despite the terror pumping through my veins, but the hatred in their eyes only burns brighter as they hit me with their favorite curse, "Otherfucker!"

Thornn pushes open the car door with so much force it's a miracle it doesn't fly off its hinges. Despite my order to the contrary, I'm relieved he didn't pause more than a few seconds after my request for him to stay put before he pushed his door open to rescue me.

Fear for him and deep affection rise within me when that big, green frame unfolds and he stands to his full height. With an otherworldly battle cry, he joins the fray, his orcish strength evident as he grapples with one of the attackers, keeping out of the striking zone of the nail-studded board.

It's terrifying and fascinating to watch the male who touches me with heartrending gentle caresses, fight like a barbarian warrior against our attackers.

My heart races as I watch the chaotic struggle. With the clash of limbs and shouts of hatred thick in the air, my hands tremble as I wonder if either of us will make it out alive. Right now, he's keeping the assholes at bay, but I worry that even if we escape in one piece, if anyone gets in legal trouble from this melee, it will be the green Other, not the local human punks.

Although I wish I could help, I back up, half-hidden by the gas pump, my phone at my ear, desperate to hear the voice of a 911 operator. My breaths come in ragged gasps, the world around me a blur of aggression and chaos.

"911, what's your emergency?" A voice crackles through my phone, but my attention is consumed by the unfolding brawl. I manage to relay the name of the gas station and the nature of the attack, hoping the urgency in my voice speaks volumes.

Seconds later, the distant wailing of sirens pierces through the chaos. The attackers, realizing the police will be here in seconds, scatter like roaches in the light. My relief is palpable, but the damage is done. I'm shaken to the core as I visually inspect Thornn for damage. He hurries to my side and protectively throws his arms around me. His chest heaves as he hugs me tight.

"Are you okay?" he husks. "I wanted to help you sooner. Why did you order me to stay in the car?"

"To keep you safe." I pull back enough to look into his precious face, then skim my hands over his shoulders and down his arms.

As I notice a tear near the shoulder of his hoodie and search beneath to see a bloody scratch, he husks, his voice full of pain, "My job is to keep *you* safe, Sarah. Not the other way around."

Although I was terrified during the attack, the weight of what happened hits me like a sledgehammer. We could have both been killed.

"I just..." I'm trembling so hard, he pulls me tight and strokes my hair. "I couldn't bear to see you hurt. Just c-couldn't."

"Don't you see? It killed me to stay inside while you were in harm's way. I'll never forgive myself for leaving you alone outside the car for even one minute, although you ordered me to stay safe. I couldn't stand by and watch them touch a hair on your head."

"Thanks for not following my ridiculous order, Thornn." He really did save my life just then. I wonder when my racing heart will come back to normal. "It was a no-win situation."

As the police arrive, the world slows down. Thornn and I exchange a glance, a silent understanding passing between us. This was more than a physical assault; it was an attack on his very being, on my safety, and just might have destroyed what we have together.

Thornn already knew how dangerous the world can be, learned it at the end of a Purist's blade when he was attacked. Today was my first lesson, a bone-deep knowledge that it's impossible for either of us to stay safe in this relationship. It's a bitter awakening.

CHAPTER THIRTY

T hornn

I thought having only one ball was the worst thing that could happen to a male, the broken tusk and shorn hair coming in a distant second. But sitting in that fucking car, watching my female get attacked, was the worst thing that has happened in my life—bar none. As emasculated as I feel right now, someone might as well cut off my other ball.

The police all but accused me of starting things with those criminals, but after Sarah and I repeated what happened twenty times, both of our stories staying the same, they let us go.

Perhaps it had something to do with the spiked stick the attackers dropped on the ground as they ran away. The damage to Sarah's vehicle and the many scratch marks that match the nails also corroborated our story.

An uncomfortable silence hangs thick between Sarah and me as she pulls out of the gas station parking lot. She opens her mouth to speak, but the words seem to stick in her throat. I turn, pretending to look out the side window, as my mind still reels from the attack.

"Do you want me to drive?" I ask, though I'm distracted.

I failed her. Although she practically ordered me to stay in the car, I should have intervened earlier. What kind of male lets his female protect him? If any of my friends knew how I let

CHAPTER THIRTY

her down, put her in danger... well, they wouldn't be my friends anymore.

"No. It will do me good to drive. Keep my mind off..." Her hands are trembling.

"What if I insisted?" I ask with a thrust of my chin.

"Thornn, trust me, I'd rather stay busy."

Other than arm wrestling her, I have no recourse but to let her drive, which just highlights my impotence.

The car rockets forward, the highway stretching out ahead, but the atmosphere inside the cab is heavy with the unspoken weight of the violence we just endured.

The concern in Sarah's eyes deepens as she cuts me quick glances. I feel a pang of guilt, an ache that goes beyond the physical. She deserves better than this. Deserves better than a life entangled with me and everything I represent.

"Thornn, are you..." Her voice falters, and for a moment, I see the genuine worry etched across her features.

Am I okay? The question hangs in the air, a heavy weight I can't easily shake off. How can I be okay when so many people seem to hate my very existence? How can I be okay when every step forward is a battle against a society that hates me?

"I'm... I'll be fine," I manage to mumble, my voice barely audible even to myself. Those words tasted bitter on my tongue.

We continue in uneasy silence, the road becoming a monotonous backdrop to my inner war. Sarah makes a few more attempts at conversation, but my responses become increasingly monosyllabic. My mind is a battleground, torn between the growing affection I feel for her and the fear that I'll become more of a liability with every passing day.

She reaches out to touch my hand, a gesture of comfort, but I flinch involuntarily.

"Sorry," I say, instantly regretting my actions. "I just..."

"Should we stop driving early? Rent a motel room? Shake this off?"

"No!" That came out harsh, but the last thing I want is to prolong this trip.

I steal a glance at her, her beautiful profile somehow unmarred from today's ugly events. The vulnerability in her eyes tugs at my heart.

After pulling into a rest area, she turns off the engine, and the silence becomes almost suffocating. I can feel her gaze on me, waiting for me to open up, to share the pain that I carry. But how can I burden her with the dark shit lurking inside me, coiling around my guts like a living thing?

She undoes her seatbelt and turns to look at me. Perhaps that doesn't meet her need for connection, because she cups her palm to my cheek and manages a wan smile.

"Nothing has changed for me, Thornn. Nothing. I should have told you days ago. I was just too chickenshit to be the first to say it, but I love you. It's the biggest emotion I've ever felt."

She pauses so her words hit home. I'm glad she waited, because for a moment I didn't understand the magnitude of her words. When she sees the dawning of understanding in my expression, she nods.

"That's right. My love is a bigger emotion than fear." Her eyes flash wide as though it's only now she realizes the weight of her own statement. "Fuck those assholes." After pausing for effect, she repeats, "Fuck them! I am not going to let them ruin this. What we've found is too precious. I've waited all my life to find someone to love, someone as wonderful as you. I'm not going to let four assholes at some shitty gas station in the middle of nowhere steal that from me."

Her hand is no longer gentle on my cheek. She's gripping my shoulder, urging me to look her square in the face.

"Do you hear me? I'm not letting them steal you from me. And..." She gives my shoulder a little squeeze. "Unless you want to break up because you don't share my affection, I'm not letting *you* steal this from me, either."

"I..."

"So take your time and deal with the violence, the shit that just happened, and then move on, because what we just endured has nothing to do with us. Do you hear me?"

I palm my mouth; the gesture serving the dual purpose of soothing my emotions as well as hiding them.

Damn her, but she's right. Letting four teenage jerks change the trajectory of the amazing thing that's blossoming between Sarah and me isn't just stupid. It's insanity.

"Why are you always right?" I grip her by the nape and pull her closer, kissing her with a passion that has nothing to do with sex. It's fervent and earnest and powerful. "I should have told you days ago. I've never felt this way before. I love you, Sarah."

We hug for a long time, and it doesn't surprise me when the woman I love begins to cry. I'm not sure whether it's a delayed reaction to the attack or from the relief of my declaration of love. Perhaps a little of both.

I sway with her as I kiss the top of her head, her temples, her cheeks. Then I purr. It does its job, calming her, soothing her. She leans far enough away to slide her hand between us so her palm presses on my chest. Hearing my purr, feeling its vibration makes her hum with pleasure.

"You're right. That purr is magic." She nuzzles my neck, her warm breath ghosting across my flesh.

"You're going to switch places with me and I'm going to drive through the night if I have to. We're going to wind up at your condo, if you'll let me, since I'm currently homeless. No matter where I sleep tonight, I'm going to talk to Chief Brokka tomorrow after a good night's sleep. I'll get my job back, become a productive, *speaking* member of society, and be the best male I can be so that I deserve you, Sarah."

I pause a moment, waiting for her to pull away so we can switch places. When those Colorado-blue-sky eyes finally gaze into mine, I add, "You make me want to be a better male."

CHAPTER THIRTY-ONE

S arah

"We pulled in at dawn and it's not even noon. You should sleep in," Thornn says as he kisses the most delicious spot behind my ear. "I'm wide awake, though, and want to talk to Chief Brokka right away about getting back on active duty."

His hand is possessively on my hip as he spoons me from behind. "Why don't you sleep until I return? I'll bring back breakfast. There are the most amazing Other burritos called *timplatos* I'll buy from the naga female who sells them on the street corner near the fire station. Can I borrow your car?"

I burrow back against him, luxuriating in his heat. Is it my fault I accidentally rub my bottom against his morning wood?

"Don't start what you can't finish, Sarah." There's a commanding edge to his voice. "I owe you an explanation about why I've kept one of my *biggest assets* away from you." He grinds against me as he speaks, then jacks his ass back, perhaps following his own advice not to start what he can't finish. "Tonight, when we're both well rested, I'll tell you everything I should have told you weeks ago and perhaps I'll give you... a guided tour?"

He's behind me. How is it I know he's doing that silly-sexy eyebrow-waggling thing?

"Why wait?" I wiggle again and my arousal spikes higher when I feel his enormous cock jerk beneath his sleep pants.

"Because you, my dear, should grab some more sleep while you can. We should be in peak form to accomplish all the things I want to do with you later."

"I could get in peak form right this minute. I just need a little revving up." Who am I kidding? I don't need any revving. I'm ready now, especially since my interest is piqued about what he's been withholding in the bedroom. I assumed he didn't want to terrify me with his size, although his sweats leave little to the imagination when he's aroused.

"Nope." He scoots back and pats my backside before he eases off the bed. "I don't want to wait a minute more to get back on the force. I may not have a lot to bring to the table, but you should at least have a partner who works."

He pauses, a thoughtful expression on his face, then steps closer and leans to give a soft pecking kiss to the spot on my bottom that he just swatted. "A partner who works, and *who loves you.*" He lances me with a sincere, molten look, then rummages in his bag for his toothbrush.

My mind wanders to the future as I imagine this type of fun interactions and exchanges of morning intimacies for years to come. Since it's clear that bedroom activities are off the table for this morning, I call, "I'm coming with you."

He strides into the bedroom with his sleep pants slung low on his hips, looking better than he has any right to after yesterday's ordeal and so little sleep.

"Not that I don't want you, but why don't you catch up on your sleep? The last month has been hell in a lot of ways. You deserve a break."

"I want to talk to Emma. She works from home; I know I'll catch her."

"Do you need to ask if you're crazy to be in a relationship with me?" While he tries to sound casual, as though he's kidding, I

CHAPTER THIRTY-ONE

can read him well enough to know the question isn't really a joke.

Forcing myself out of bed, I kiss the side of his cheek that's pooched out because his toothbrush is jammed in it.

"No. I don't need her pronouncement about my sanity. I want to brag about how terrific you are." He kisses me, smearing a few minty suds on my lips. "Go spit! I'll drive us to the Zone, drop you at the firehouse, and barge in on my friend. If you're nice, I'll stop at Maxx's Coffee and get you your favorite when I buy Emma a caramel cappuccino as payment for listening to me drone on about all your *assets*."

"Okay. But if places were reversed, you can bet your adorable ass I'd jump at the chance to sleep in."

Half an hour later, I pull up to Maxx's, leave the car running, and dart inside to pick up my online order.

When I return to the car, I open the door behind my seat and bend to place the small holder carrying three coffees on the floor. I'm fumbling, trying not to get run over, knowing my open door is sticking into the busy four-lane street.

Somehow, the car's Bluetooth grabs onto some texts that must have come in while I was in the coffee shop. With the phone in my purse and my hands full, the last four texts come through in a row, each preceded by a ping, then the computerized voice's monotone announcement.

Ping: *Honey, Dad and I just got off the boat and a bunch of your texts came in at once. I can't tell you how upset we are to hear the news.*

Ping: *An orc? An Other? Did we raise you wrong? Is this your way of getting back at us for something? Is it your walk on the wild side? Late blooming teenage rebellion?*

In my crazy haste to get to my phone, I dump almost an entire cup of Thornn's black coffee on the back of my hand. I howl in pain as I set the container down and try to dig in my purse for the phone before another heinous text comes through—

Ping: *Sarah? This is your dad. Did we read your last few texts correctly? You were attacked by a gang? Because of that orc?*

"Turn off the radio. Turn off the volume!" I shout to Thornn, though it's too late to fix what he's already heard. I barely feel what are probably first-degree burns on my hand; my mind is totally focused on what Thornn just heard and how he must be feeling right now. My head already hurts, my stomach is in knots, and I feel my life spiraling out of control.

Though those texts must have broken Thornn's heart, I'll explain that I'm a grown woman and my parents don't dictate who I can and cannot love.

Ping: *We're cutting our trip short and are catching the first plane out of Leonardo da Vinci Airport. Going to talk some sense into you to keep you from ruining your life.*

The blare of a car horn reminds me that my ass is still sticking out into the street, so I leave the mess on the floor, manage to make my way into the driver's seat, and close the door behind me without getting run over. My body may not have been run over, but I feel like I've been hit by a Mack truck. From one moment to the next, my entire life just changed.

CHAPTER THIRTY-TWO

Thornn

My brain has quit working. Nothing like this has happened to me before, even right before I lost consciousness during the Purist attack. I'm simply floating in so many feelings—shitty feelings—that Thornn is gone. I'm just an observer of what's happening.

When I finally return to my body and my brain sparks back to life, Sarah is out of the street and behind the wheel. Her gaze seeks mine, but I can't look at her. I'm big and strong and courageous enough that I left the protection of the Zone to rescue Emma and Kam during that riot. Yet I don't have the balls to look at the woman I love right now.

I'd leave the car this moment, but we're miles from the Zone and walking from here to there would be dangerous. I don't know if I can keep my sanity through another attack. Not after yesterday. I'll just hang in here, saying nothing until we drive through the gates. I'll pretend nothing's wrong until she drops me at the station, then I'll never see her again.

"That must have been terrible to hear, but Thornn, we'll get through this. I'll talk to them, make them understand. When they meet you, they'll see the giant heart that lives inside you. They would have to be blind not to see how good you are for me."

She reaches to grab my hand, but this time when I flinch from her, it's intentional.

Less than a minute ago, I decided to play along with her until she takes me to the fire station, but something snaps inside me at her insistence that everything is okay. Maybe it's not a snap. It's more of an explosion where everything I've built up in my mind comes crashing down in the span of a second.

"Sure, do it now. Call them. Tell them how great our relationship will be. How you, an *heiress*, owner of mansions and bearer bonds and multiple diamond cocktail rings, are going to have a really great life living in the heart of the Integration Zone. They'll love picturing you living in a tenement built in the 50s that hasn't been upgraded since then. Go ahead, Sarah, tell them."

I'm shaking. I don't know if it's rage or pain or some emotion that has never been discovered before but is so deep and hot and painful that it has no name and can't be contained.

"No, no, it won't be like that." Her protest is as weak as her argument.

"Yeah, give them a call." My decision to handle this calmly was a fool's errand. I'm completely out of control. "What time did we pull up to your condo this morning?"

She falters, eyes wide, sightless as she appears to debate whether my question was rhetorical or if I really want an answer. I spare her the effort of figuring it out.

"We arrived just after 5:00 AM. Do you remember how we *snuck* in and didn't even bring all of your suitcases from the car?"

"That was because it was five in the morning."

"And it was also because you wanted to get the great big giant green orc from the car to your condo without anyone noticing him and freaking out and causing another scene. Tell me, Sarah, how will that work in the long term?"

"We can move out of the condo, to a house with more land."

CHAPTER THIRTY-TWO 137

My fury is ebbing, swiftly being replaced by a blank hole in the pit of my stomach, but I keep pressing to ensure she gets the picture.

"Right. Yeah, let's move. Why don't you take all the money you just inherited and move farther away from the Zone where I still won't be able to walk from the car to the house without upsetting the neighbors? I won't be able to even leave the house to jog around the block, Sarah. We'll never be able to go to a restaurant or on a hike or a ride in the car without risk. What's that life going to be like, huh?"

Maybe she's picturing it, the life she'll have with me. A lifetime of arguing with parents and well-meaning friends who think she's throwing her life away for me. Years of hiding because if we go anywhere together we might be attacked.

I see awareness dawning on her beautiful face, her sadness apparent in the tears falling down her cheeks. I hate to take pleasure in her pain, but that she's sad at our breakup is the best thing that's happened to me this morning. At least when I look back on this for years to come, I'll know that even for one brief, shining moment, she truly cared for me.

"Thornn, I fell fast and hard for you, but that doesn't make it any less powerful or any less real. I love you deeply and want to spend my life with you. We'll find a way to make this work."

It's as though the heavens open up and a beam of light shines directly into my brain as I realize what I have to do right now. For her sake. I must stomp on her heart, scorch the Earth, make sure that all her feelings for me are crushed and obliterated so she can move forward and never look back.

"It was fucking delusional to believe this could possibly work. I've got to give you credit, Sarah. I think you were fucking delusional, too. When you give it one thought in the cold, hard light of day, it's obvious this will never work."

Throwing all control to the wind, I string all my faults into a list and recite them for her.

"I'm an orc without any advanced education who isn't currently employed and you're a brilliant, beautiful, witty, accomplished woman who deserves far better than a tuskless, male from another species from another world."

Stricken. The stricken expression on her face, wide-eyed, open-mouthed, and full of pain, tells me my message was received. Perhaps a little bit of hatred is beginning to simmer inside her. Good. It will help her get over me, because the Goddess only knows how I'm ever going to get over her.

"You're going to start this car and take me to the Zone just as we planned. You'll drop me at the firehouse and arrange with Emma to get me my clothes. And Sarah?"

Her attention was fading as my words seemed to be hitting internally like depth charges. Using her name brought her attention back so I can ensure she hears my next statement.

"We are never going to see each other again. And—"

It's only now that I look down to see her hand is red.

"What the fuck happened to your hand?"

Gently, I grip her forearm, inches from her damaged skin. Without conscious thought, I pull her hand to my face and lick it. Orc saliva has healing properties. My friends who are mated to humans have mentioned it works on them, too.

"S-spilled the coffee..."

Our gazes meet as I lick the back of her hand, her fingers, and the spaces between them. Less than a minute ago I was giving her my final ultimatum, vowing we'd never see each other again, and now our gazes are locked and the movements of my tongue are reminding us both of the intimacies we shared in our bed as the scent of pines wafted through our bedroom screens.

Dear Goddess, how will I be able to continue to live? To continue to breathe in and out and wake and go to sleep and know that I will never again see the precious woman who even now, even after I just flayed her alive with my words, is looking

CHAPTER THIRTY-TWO

at me with love and adoration. Adoration after the shit I just spewed at her.

I drag my glance away, forcing myself to focus on healing her hand. We can't continue, can't see each other again, although both our hearts are breaking. I wouldn't be able to live with myself if I ruined her life.

"You'll forget me. Move on. We knew each other for barely a month. In another month, this will be a faded memory," I lie. Maybe the pain will disappear for her, but it will *never* fade for me.

Why does the Goddess mock me? Why at this very moment do I see Sarah in a flickering red haze, telling me she might be my soulbound mate? When orcs become soulbound, they see their beloved in a red haze. From what my father told me, the red haze happens only with shared bliss after declaring deep, abiding love and commitment.

It's just the faintest color, and perhaps I'm just imagining it. Somehow, though, I think the Goddess is telling me Sarah's my soulbound. What terrible timing.

She's wearing a look of abject pain, her lips parted with a half-spoken word, tears running down her face and wetting the fabric of her blouse, and her dark hair is falling out of her messy bun, and the red haze that surrounds her fills the air like the Northern Lights.

The Goddess has a terrible sense of humor, soulbonding me to a woman I've just vowed to never see again.

CHAPTER THIRTY-THREE

One-hundred Days Later...

Thornn

I should read my most recent text again. It shook me to my core. Instead, I scroll up, watching one hundred texts from Sarah fly by until I arrive at the first one she sent the day after she dropped me at the fire station, then pulled away upon my command that we never see each other again.

I brought all your belongings back to the Zone last night. They're at Kam and Emma's. I told my parents not to cut their vacation short because I won't see them. Not after what they said about you. Can I see you today? Maybe I can explain better.

I didn't respond, nor have I responded to any of the ninety-nine texts that have come through once a day since then. Well, that's not entirely true. When I got my new tusk implant, I sent her pictures the dentist took of me.

I wasn't smiling. My text simply said, *This wouldn't have been possible without the money you loaned me. I'll be forever grateful. Now that I've paid you back from the wages you gave me, I think it's best we don't communicate even by text anymore.*

CHAPTER THIRTY-THREE

Her response was, *I'm so, so thrilled that you got your tusk replaced. I hope it makes you feel better about yourself. You look amazing, by the way.*

She continued to send one text a day, but after my one text to her, I never responded—not once.

But after the one I just received, I'll be forced to respond.

I scroll through the first seven she sent as she politely asked in various ways to see me, wanting to explain. They were all loaded with apologies, which squeezed at my already broken heart, because none of this is her fault. She has nothing to apologize for.

Perhaps I should have told her that, reassured her that this wasn't her fault. Except I knew if I'd responded, it would have started a dangerous precedent that would only hurt us both in the end.

After the first week, the brief, perky updates started coming through.

Taking time off at Aunt Beth's house helped me with my dissertation from hell. For one, my respite means I don't hate Shakespeare anymore. Taking a break did wonders for our relationship.

I couldn't tell if that was a hint about her and me, or if it was about her relationship with the Bard of Avon.

I've been vacillating about whether to put Beth's place up for sale (I wonder if it will always be Beth's place to me or if one day it will feel like mine). In the meantime, I'll leave it alone. Sooz and her crew will come monthly to clean and give me a report on any problems.

Each of her newsy texts stole endless minutes of my life as I read and re-read and looked between the lines to see if there were hidden messages for me. All of her texts about the house in Colorado made my thoughts arrow to the hours we spent together. It's as though everything that happened there, except the stench, was bathed in a golden glow of remembered happiness.

Finished my dissertation!!!!! Yes, Thornn, five exclamation marks. And here are five more!!!!! This feels monumental.

My excitement for her was so powerful it was as though we were still in a relationship. Yet, I didn't respond.

Met with my advisor today. He certainly didn't lavish me with praise. At least all his suggestions will keep me busy for a while.

That wasn't subtle at all. She was trying to keep busy, to keep from feeling the pain of her loss. I know the feeling.

My meeting with Dr. Culp went better today. He approves of the direction I'm heading with the dissertation. Feeling confident!

Each day it was as though I was going through this with her, as I silently celebrated each of her wins and mourned all her losses.

It's been a month. I'm hoping you've had enough time to get your life back in order. Kam tells me you're back on the force. Go you! And I was so glad to hear the Zone Housing Authority found you a place to live. I imagine it feels great to be in your own place again. I wonder if you're ready to meet with me. To hear how sorry I am. Maybe we could try again?

That one hurt. In fact, it hurts now as I re-read it. I can feel her pain, though we're miles away. No one likes to grovel, but she did it. And I didn't respond.

After that, she went back to her chatty updates. Her dissertation was always a topic of concern, it clearly consumed her waking hours. Sometimes there were upbeat mentions of a new show she was binge-watching. Those always ended with either, *I think you might like this one*, or, *Don't bother watching... you'd hate it*.

After a while, it quit surprising me when I'd jump on the Internet, watch the trailer, and find that her assessment of my likes and dislikes was one hundred percent accurate. We may have only been together for a month, but she knows me well.

CHAPTER THIRTY-THREE

A few weeks ago, her daily text had very few words, but I could feel the emotion though we were miles apart.

I've got a date to defend my dissertation. Five weeks to prepare. YIKES!

When I met her, I knew nothing about doctoral theses or dissertations or defending them, but over the long days as we dispatched clutter and cobwebs, I became intimately acquainted with every aspect of the process. The text about her date to defend her dissertation sounded terrified, justifiably so. She needed an encouraging word, yet I held firm and didn't respond.

Which is why today's text surprised me more than it should have. I knew this day would come, had been dreading it and looking forward to it in equal measure. I just thought I had more time.

Now that I've scrolled through all one hundred texts, I've caught up to the one I received this morning.

The day I dropped you off at the firehouse, I came home, cried my eyes out, and counted out exactly one hundred days on the calendar. I vowed that I would do everything in my power, while honoring your boundaries, to fix things between us. To make things work.

For the first time since this started, her message is so long it comes through in more than one part.

Today is day one hundred. You won't hear from me after today. So, I'm taking a big risk and asking for something I want. Until now, I've put your feelings ahead of mine.

Reading that sentence makes my heart clench. She shouldn't have to do that.

Today, I'm asking (well, begging really) to meet you face to face. To speak with you. To get closure. Emma tells me there's a park at Blemmins and Vine inside the Zone. Name the time and I'll be there. I'd really like this chance to clear things up in my own head, but I'll understand and respect your wishes if you don't want to.

I didn't know bodies could respond this way, but my chest feels as though it's exploding and imploding at the same time. The effect is that for a moment I can't breathe at all.

I should let this text go, just as I have all the others, without a response. But that's a shit thing to do. Sarah never asked, not once since the first text, to meet. This obviously means a lot to her, and I simply can't ignore her request. Nor can I deny her.

Perhaps it's because I need the closure, too. Goddess knows not a waking hour has gone by that I haven't thought of the woman who owns my very heart and soul. Sadly, those thoughts are always tempered with reminders that things between us will never work.

Yes. I'll see you at seven if it works for you.

I type, *Don't get your hopes up. Nothing will change.* Then back out of it. No reason to crush her spirit. There will be a lifetime of that after we part ways tonight.

CHAPTER THIRTY-FOUR

T hornn

My breath catches as I spot Sarah across the cracked blacktop. Even after months apart, her beauty steals my air. Chestnut waves bounce gently around her face as she approaches. Our eyes meet and the world falls away. In that endless moment, only she exists.

As she nears, details imprint: jeans hugging her hips, a flowing blouse with purple swirls, her bottom teeth gnawing her upper lip. Her piercing, sky-blue gaze connects with mine for the swiftest moment, then skitters away as though this barren wasteland of a park is the most fascinating thing she's ever seen.

Fear. She's terrified of this meeting. Terrified of my rejection. Although I try, my gaze flies to the nearby swing set, because she should be terrified. I am going to reject her. I have no choice. I have nothing to give her. Nothing she needs. Nothing she deserves.

The sturdy, blue backpack over her shoulder seems heavy. Did I leave some of my belongings at her house? I thought I got everything; I only spent one night.

The last time we spoke, I was so harsh to her. My words were designed to wake her up, make her see the reality of how circumstances were stacked against us. Despite the wrecking ball of our last conversation, here she is.

"Hello, Thornn."

Her lyrical voice bathes me in warmth. I thought I'd successfully buried my desire for her, my love for her, but it's bursting through me, flowing in my veins like warm honey. It was misguided to hope that since we didn't actually consummate the soulbond the connection would fade. I was wrong about that, too.

Halting in front of me, sorrow shadows her eyes. My hands fist, fighting the urge to caress her soft skin. Those nights we shared in the master bedroom, I learned so many things about her body. How a feather-soft brush on the inside of her elbow made her gasp. How when I kissed her, if I tugged her silken hair just this side of rough, her gaze would fly to me, her lids would shut, and then she'd give me that shy smile that was my favorite, as though she was asking for more.

I shove those treasonous thoughts out of my head as I wait for her to speak. She requested this meeting. The charged moment stretches taut.

Finally, she murmurs, "I've missed you."

My throat tightens, emotion threatening to choke me. The reality of having her near again is almost too much to bear. I swallow, tamping down my emotions. It's best to let her have her say, get the closure she wants and needs, and then leave, knowing I'll never see or hear from her again.

I desperately want to tell her I've missed her, too. That I lie awake until the wee hours of the night thinking about her, rewinding every minute of our time together and replaying it in delicious, addictive slow motion. I want to tell her how sometimes I catch a scent of flowers on the breeze and close my eyes, imagining she's in the next room.

I want to tell her I've been reading Shakespeare and though I still can't say I love him like she does, I'm learning to appreciate him. Well, that's a lie. But I'm tolerating him better. She'd be proud of me. But my desire to hear her praise would be a dead giveaway of just how much I still care about her, which would do neither of us any good.

Instead of letting all of that pass my lips, I simply say, "I hope this meeting gives you the closure you're hoping for." Goddess, saying that made my guts clench as though they're tied in a knot.

She clears her throat as her face falls from quiet expectation to a look of resignation. She sets her backpack on the battered picnic table and throws her shoulders back as though she's about to face an enemy.

"I've replayed our last conversation in my mind a hundred times." She slides onto the seat across from me. "That's a lie. It's more like a thousand."

For the first time in a hundred days, she looks directly into my eyes. Goddess, help me. How am I going to manage this conversation without leaning over the table, begging her to take me back, and pulling her into a scorching kiss?

"I knew I needed this meeting. But I'll admit, I lied to you. I didn't request this meeting for closure. To be honest, I'm going to use it to plead my case one last time."

She reaches toward my hand, which is resting on the peeling green wood slat of the table. She snatches her hand away before she touches me. At least she's trying to observe my boundaries. Of course she is. Everything about her is so damned admirable. *That's why you're ending things,* I remind myself. *Because she deserves better, better than you.*

"I know that nothing I say will convince you that we can weather the storms that will face us. But I thought perhaps if I give you examples of how other people managed adversity, it might help you see that we can overcome our obstacles, too. Even though the problems we face seem insurmountable."

Out of her backpack, she pulls out a well-worn leather-bound book and gently lays it on the table, as though it's precious to her.

"First edition of *Twelfth Night*. My parents bought it for me when I was in junior high. It's what began my first love affair—with William Shakespeare. Perhaps if I tell you the plot, it will help me navigate my second love affair... with you."

I've pulled my hands into my lap to keep myself from touching her. Perhaps to self-soothe without my touch, she pets the cover as though it were a lover.

"This book is about several couples who stumble and bumble their way through hardships, mistaken identities, and misunderstandings, but with resilience and creativity in the face of adversity, they make it to the finish line with their love intact."

With a heavy thud, she sets another book on top of the first and says, "*Pride and Prejudice*. The hero and heroine's temperaments are polar opposites. He has arrogant pride, and she's full of prejudice, but their true characters shine through to find an enduring love."

As I regard Sarah's animated features, hope sparks inside me. If these characters she loves so much persevered and triumphed, could we also, despite the odds?

Next, she adds another book to the growing stack, then details the passionate connection between the brooding, mysterious Rochester and kind, yet ostracized governess Jane in *Jane Eyre*.

"Their bond survives even the revelation of Rochester's mad wife locked in the attic." She cocks an eyebrow at me and adds, "I admit, that one takes the cake. It's even more daunting than a love affair between an orc and a human."

As I gaze into Sarah's earnest eyes, her unwavering faith that what we've found is worth fighting for makes me ache to try again.

Sarah goes on eagerly, telling the sweeping tale of Westley's undying love for Buttercup in *The Princess Bride*. Even when separated by oceans and reported as dead, Westley returns to save her, persevering through pain and misfortune. My pulse leaps, thinking of myself in his place, the depths I would go to for a chance with my darling Sarah.

CHAPTER THIRTY-FOUR

As she pulls book after book out of her bulging backpack, she threatens, "I could go on for an hour, relating stories of star-crossed lovers who found a way to stay together. Some travel through time like *The Time Traveler's Wife* or space like *Starman*."

As she straightens the stack of books, she says, "Sometimes, when I think about you so hard I know I'll never get to sleep, I get lost in the wonder of how you and I found each other. From what I understand, you Others might have traveled through time or space—maybe both—to come to Earth. And yet you found me, Thornn. We found each other. I think we're a miracle."

My heart lurches in my chest as I feel her words to the depth of me. A miracle. Isn't it true? What else explains how two such different people found each other, connected, and managed to fall in love?

My hands are tightly clenched under the table, so instead of reaching for my hand, she lays hers on the table, palms up, in invitation.

"I told my parents to fuck themselves."

My gaze darts to her in shock. This isn't the gentle Sarah I know.

"Well, not in those words. But I told them I was an adult and irrevocably in love with you and did not require their permission or approval on who I choose to love."

She spears me with her gaze, daring me to defy her statement.

"When they returned from their travels, we had a long discussion. I told them that if you and I got together, they would either accept you and be polite or they would never see me, or any children I might have, again."

It feels as though a white-hot poker stabs me through and through. I can't say I didn't think about reuniting with Sarah a million times in the last three months. Nor can I say I didn't think of us having orclings, just as a few of the human-orc couples have done here in the Zone—Emma is ready to give birth any moment. But that Sarah has not only contemplated it, but seems to want to have younglings with me. Well, the idea is both terrifying and tempting.

"So, whether my parents accept you or not is of no consequence to our relationship. I would hate to lose them, but the fact is, Thornn, I'm willing to give them up. For you."

My mind is swirling, and my body is leaning forward as though I'm pulled to her by a gravitational force. Still, that's not the only thing standing in my way of saying yes, of reuniting with her. My mere presence put her in danger at that gas station. I don't want to be the reason this amazing, perfect female is hurt. More important than my happiness—or hers—is to protect her.

I'm going to shut this conversation down. For her own good. Then I'll go home and for the rest of my life, I'll regret what I just lost.

CHAPTER THIRTY-FIVE

Sarah

I can tell I haven't swayed him, though he still loves me. That's clear from the earnest way he's listened to every word I've said, how he's leaned closer as though his mind may not want to reconcile, but his body can't stay away.

I've been planning this conversation for months, ever since he wouldn't relent in his edict that we end our relationship. I still have more to say.

Perhaps it's a good sign that although he's kept his hands in his lap until now, he sets them on the table. It's all the invitation I need to grasp Thornn's large hands in mine as I gaze earnestly into his tawny eyes. My heartbeat thrums in my ears, emotions swirling within me. I know this is my last chance to change his mind. My whole future is riding on this.

"Thornn," I begin, my voice trembling but firm. "I understand why you think ending this is for the best. I know you want to protect me from the cruelty of others, from the challenges we'll face being together. But love—true love—isn't about playing it safe. Real love requires sacrifice. It means weathering hardships side-by-side and facing problems together instead of running away."

He opens his mouth to interrupt, but I squeeze his hands, silently begging him to let me continue.

"I know being together won't be easy. We'll likely face more obstacles than most. But when I look inside my heart, none of that matters. What I feel for you eclipses everything else. Everything." I pause, blinking back sudden tears. "'I do love nothing in the world so well as you—is not that strange?' It's a quote from the boyfriend I jilted for you, William Shakespeare."

The words I quoted from *Much Ado About Nothing* hang poignantly between us. Thornn's stoic expression softens almost imperceptibly. Could my impassioned plea be getting through to him? Pressing onward, I'm bolstered by a glimmer of hope.

"I've thought this through, Thornn. I'm fully aware of what I'm signing up for. Maybe we'll never be able to stroll hand-in-hand through a park without sideways glances. Perhaps we'll always need to be vigilant in public. But we'll create a haven of our own, a space where we can just be ourselves."

I picture us snuggled together on Aunt Beth's porch bed, gazing out over the sweeping mountain vista, safe in our love. Determination wells up inside me.

"I'm willing to make whatever sacrifices our relationship requires, because being with you is worth it. Think of Kam and Emma. They make it work every single day. If they can be happy despite the prejudice, then so can we."

His upper lip curls as he replies, "You make it sound like we're the heroes of our own stories, but an Orc could never be a hero. You've picked pretty examples, I may not look it, but I read, too. Orpheus and Eurydice, Catherine and Heathcliff, Gatsby, Tess and Angel. History is littered with lovers who made a stupid decision and paid with their lives."

"Okay. You have literary examples of loving disasters, I have examples of love triumphing. The question is, what will you and I make of this beautiful connection we've stumbled into?"

CHAPTER THIRTY-FIVE

I hold his intense gaze, willing him to change his mind despite his chilling examples of the terrible fates love can wreak. His eyes shimmer, his expression torn. I know his objections aren't because he doesn't love me back just as fiercely as I love him. Leaning forward to cup his beautiful cheek, I pour all the earnest emotion I can into my words.

"I choose you, Thornn. I'll choose you every day for the rest of my life, if you let me. We belong together. Of that, I have no doubt."

His hand covers mine where it rests against his face. The rough warmth of his skin sparks something inside me that pierces to the very heart of me.

"Sarah," he rasps, raw emotion lacing his voice. "You deserve so much more than a life hidden away for my sake."

Despite the regret shadowing his handsome features, hope leaps inside me. His words don't carry the finality of our last painful conversation. Sensing I'm getting through to him, I push harder.

"That's for me to decide, isn't it?" I counter gently. "Please Thornn, take a chance on us. On this rare, wonderful thing between us. I know our path won't be easy, but with you by my side, I can weather any storm."

I hold my breath, pulse racing. Thornn gazes at me for a long moment, the battle raging inside him is etched on his beautiful green face.

"What will you do when packs of humans throw things at us in the streets, or spit in our food? No ivy league university will employ an Otherfucker, Sarah. What will you do when the Purists burn our house down around us?"

I meet his challenging gaze and reply with absolute confidence, "Well, it's a good thing my lover is a damn excellent firefighter."

Finally, he stands, rounds the edge of the table and pulls me into a crushing embrace. Joy explodes through me as he whispers gruffly, "I can deny you nothing, my stubborn, darling Sarah.

If you still want this ornery orc, knowing full well what you're getting into, then... I'm yours."

Tears spill down my cheeks as he sits backward on my side of the table after pulling me into his arms. I cling to him, believing for the first time in months that we might make this work after all.

CHAPTER THIRTY-SIX

Thornn

Nothing has felt this good in my life. Not when I passed my exam to be a firefighter, not even when I saved that elderly minotaur's life in an apartment fire. Nothing.

With Sarah finally in my arms, with all my resistance gone, my heart is soaring. Breathing in her delicious floral scent, I memorize everything about this moment because I imagine when I'm old and gray I'll still think about the moment when all my dreams came true.

It's full dark in this barren park, two of the four streetlights are out, and the sound of the crickets is background music for our reconciliation. Sarah's scant weight is in my arms, on my lap, and my heart is bursting with so much love and happiness it could overflow the ocean.

"I figured you'd try to convince me to come back." As I press swift, soft kisses along her hairline, I drown in the joy of having her in my arms. "I'd prepared myself for it, hoping I could resist you."

Ah, to have her soft, curvy form in my arms, on my lap. I'd forgotten how magical it felt to have her so close, so dear.

"Are you saying I'm irresistible?"

I should joke, tell her she's too full of herself and needs to be brought down a peg. But I can't, even though it will give her the upper hand for the rest of our lives.

"Totally. Totally irresistible." Her lording it over me forever will be worth it. I might as well admit it. "My admission just gave you unlimited power." I twist awkwardly to press my lips softly to hers.

"That makes us even, Thornn, because I can't resist you either. I marked today's date in red a hundred days ago. As each day passed, my stomach coiled tighter because it signaled the end of my hope. I died a little every day."

Hearing her admission steals my breath, but she'll be better now. Her ordeal is over. I'm hers. Forever.

"My guts have been in a knot the entire time, too. I'm sorry. So, so sorry for ignoring one hundred texts, Sarah. I told myself a thousand times that it was for your own good. But knowing how much it hurt you tore at my guts."

"Stubborn orc." She reaches for a kiss, her lips landing on my chin.

We stay like this for long minutes, reveling in the warmth and smell of each other. Enjoying the bliss of our reconciliation.

"As long as it's time for revelations, there's something else I need to tell you."

She must feel every muscle in my body stiffen, but instead of turning cold in response, she snuggles closer, pressing her lips to my chest.

"We'll need to be looking at each other for this."

Before she hops off my lap, she says, "We just had a long discussion about weathering all storms, Thornn. Unless you're a mass murderer or have another wife or two hidden away somewhere, I have faith we'll get through this, no matter what."

CHAPTER THIRTY-SIX

She eases to the ground and rounds the table. Now she's sitting where I'd been earlier and I've claimed her spot. When she reaches across the table to hold my hands, I shake my head once, my lips pressed into a firm line.

Despite her insistence that she'll be able to handle the information I'm about to impart, I'm not so sure. My heart is pumping as though I just ran a marathon.

"Tear off the Band-Aid, Thornn. We'll pick up the pieces—together—no matter what."

I doubt it, but do as she says.

"Everyone assumed that my shutting down after being attacked was because of my tusk—"

"Which looks great, by the way. I never cared one way or the other. As handsome as you are, I never noticed. But I imagine you feel so much better now that you have your implant."

It's just like Sarah to be so sweet and positive, but I pull us back on track.

"My breakdown was about more than my hair and my tusk." When I dredge up the nerve to look at her, I'm reassured by the warmth of her glance, but I imagine it's false hope. By the way her gaze doesn't flinch from mine, it's clear she knows how hard this conversation is for me. She's with me, though, giving me strength through the sheer force of that accepting blue gaze.

"My attackers cut me with knives and pounded me with fists and when I was down, they kicked me. It was relentless. Even though I tucked myself into a tight position, they managed to reach my balls. One of them ruptured and had to be removed."

It's dark now, and quiet. Even the bugs quit their symphony as I spilled my shame. It's just me and Sarah, separated by this weathered green picnic table as she absorbs my words.

My stomach squeezes as her lids flutter closed. Shit. It's worse than I imagined. She can't even bear to look at me.

"That must have been excruciating."

That's my Sarah, focusing on how this affected me instead of her. But soon, she'll realize what this means, that I'm only half a male, and she won't be able to look at me for entirely different reasons.

"Yeah, agony. Made me pass out."

"That's why you never got naked with me, not in all the times you brought me pleasure."

I respond with one curt nod as I wait for her face to reflect the disgust that must be swirling inside her.

"I'm sorry you went through that." She reaches out to grip my hand, and although I'm waiting for her to say more, she seems content to sit in silence with me.

"And…?" I prompt her for more.

"Is there more? I know I'm getting way ahead of the plot here. I mean, we've only just gotten back together and haven't talked about marriage, much less kids. But are you saying that losing one testicle made you… unable to father children?"

"The doctor said that wouldn't be a problem."

Instead of the look of repulsion I'm waiting to see on her face, her expression is filled with confusion.

"What am I missing here, Thornn? I don't understand the problem."

Anger flares through me. Is she being deliberately obtuse? Does she need me to spell it out? Okay.

"I only have one ball, Sarah. I'm not fully a man, not a complete male."

She squints, as though that will help her see the problem better.

"You're all male to me, Thornn. And although it's too early to discuss having kids, I'm glad you can have them. I don't see the problem." Her head is tipped, her mouth slightly puckered—the picture of confusion.

For a moment, I feel as though I'm a computer that can't compute. Then I ask a few more questions, but every one of her answers indicates she couldn't care less.

"You hid yourself from me... are you saying they didn't give you a replacement?" Though there's still no disgust in her expression, what's blooming there is rage. She explains that they have things similar to breast implants for men who lose a testicle.

"I had a friend who got them for her horse after he was gelded. They give them to horses, but they didn't suggest one for *you?*" she snarls with indignation.

I explain that the surgeon was a substitute at the Zone Clinic that night. He'd never worked the Zone before or after the night he patched me up.

"Fucker!" she shouts. "Fucker knew it would make you feel less complete and didn't even *mention* fixing it. Probably a Purist. Let's put a medical consult on our list of things to do. Should we put it before or after consummating our relationship? If I get a vote, I vote after. Let's go back to your place and *consummate*, baby."

This was what I've had myself in knots about? She never blinked, never flinched, not for one moment did it appear this bothered her at all. After thanking the Goddess for bringing Sarah into my life, I scold myself for letting all those Colorado nights go by when I was too chickenshit to take off my clothes, though she begged me to.

"You know I need to be in charge in the bedroom, lovely Sarah, but on this, I'll agree with your decision. Let's consummate."

CHAPTER THIRTY-SEVEN

Sarah

I'm ready to go, but as Thonn grips my wrist, something in his eyes stops me short.

"There's one more thing I need to do before we go," he says, voice husky with emotion.

He lifts me and sits me on top of the picnic table's weathered surface. There's something about this huge, muscular male picking me up and setting me down as though I'm his plaything that heats my blood.

As he sits on the bench between my legs, I wait, curiosity piqued. His hands slide into his hair, fingers combing through the dark waves that frame his handsome features.

"Orc hair braiding is deeply meaningful in my culture. Each braid style has significance." His amber eyes find mine through the gloom. "Since the attack, since I felt so broken, so inadequate, I haven't braided my hair. But now, with you..." His voice catches and he pauses before continuing, "It's grown long enough now. I want to come to you as a whole male."

My breath catches at the intimacy of this moment. I nod wordlessly as he instructs me how to section and plait his hair into an intricate style. After he turns to face away from me on

CHAPTER THIRTY-SEVEN

the bench below me, I smooth the silken strands between my fingers. Our bond seems to strengthen with each pass and twist.

His earthy, masculine scent fills my senses, the soft slide of his hair through my fingers kindling a whole-body yearning for more of him. Although I'm desperate to get somewhere private, part of me enjoys this gentle, public intimacy, wanting to draw it out as we connect even more deeply.

We don't speak, letting the sounds of the night breeze and distant crickets wind around us. The braiding draws us close in shared ritual as the elaborate weave comes together strand by strand. His shoulders relax, tension easing from his powerful frame with my every tender touch.

As I secure the final braid in place, emotion clogs my throat at the privilege of restoring this small but meaningful piece of him. When he turns to look at me, my palms slide down to frame his beloved face. The look in his tawny eyes pierces me to my core—gratitude, wonder, naked vulnerability, and above all, love.

"And you, Sarah? Shall I braid your hair in an American style? Do you want the mark of an unmated female? Or..." his voice dips low, the look on his face filled with meaning, "shall I braid your hair as a mated female?"

"I thought you were in charge, Thornn. I think I've been pretty damn clear about my relationship status."

He gives a huff of laughter, then his large hands cup my face, angling my head to give me a kiss full of meaning and hope. Heat spirals through me, my skin tingling everywhere we touch. Just when I'm about to crawl into his lap, he gently pulls back. Confusion clouds my desire-addled brain.

"My turn," he murmurs, his gaze tender yet simmering.

We switch places, and I immediately notice the warmth of being sheltered between his knees and muscular calves.

My lips part in wonder as his strong yet infinitely gentle fingers comb through my hair. He works slowly, reverently, weaving intricate plaits close to my scalp. The sensation of him handling my heavy locks so intimately would be soothing if we weren't building toward a different, more sensual type of closeness. I cling to the sturdy muscles of his calves, awash in heady sensations.

I'm intoxicated by his nearness, his heat and strength surrounding me. Each tug on my scalp stokes the smoldering need inside.

Time seems suspended as he crafts his design strand by strand. The plaits grow heavy against my neck, symbolizing my commitment to him. When he secures the last braid, emotions choke me, the enormity of this step sinking in. I press my hands over his where they linger against my temples. Tilting my face up to his, I whisper the only words that matter.

"I love you, Thornn."

In answer, his mouth claims mine, his kiss searing in its tenderness and passion.

"I live a couple blocks away. Want a piggyback ride? Before you answer, I warn you, by the time we cross my threshold, every person in the Zone will know not only that we're back together, but exactly what our hairstyles proclaim, and they'll all have a pretty good idea of what's going on behind my front door."

My answer is to shrug into my backpack, stand on the bench and make a "come-here" motion with my hands as I prepare to climb onto his back.

"Bring it on, world. We've got nothing to hide!"

CHAPTER THIRTY-EIGHT

Thornn

I've wanted this for one hundred days. Yearned for it, despaired that I would never get it. Now that my female is in my arms—well, on my back—my heart is soaring with happiness.

At some point, I'll tell her about the soulbond. It will probably piss her off that I didn't mention it earlier, that I didn't tell her in response to her hundred texts. Despite the proof of how deep our connection is, its existence changed nothing, so I'll save the big reveal for later. After I take her to bed.

As we approach my little house, Sarah leans close to my ear to exclaim, "I thought you lived in an apartment."

"Emma calls it a happy accident that my apartment was rented out while I was... having my meltdown—"

"Existential crises," she interrupts. "It sounds so much less pathetic. Kind of hip."

"Right. Whatever. So, when I returned to the Zone after my trip to Colorado, all that was available was this little bungalow from the 1950s. It's not quite a mansion on its best day, Sarah," I hedge. "And I wasn't expecting company..."

"Does it have a *bed?*" her voice dropped suggestively.

"I can guarantee you a bed and little else."

"What more do we need?"

I may be an Other, but I've grown up on Earth. I've watched enough movies to know I'm supposed to carry my new mate over the threshold. Stopping on the cracked cement walkway that travels from the street to my front door, I squat, help her off my back, then lift her up and carry her in the position I've seen in a dozen happy endings.

"Not exactly the wedding or honeymoon of your dreams, I'm sure." I thought I'd banished my doubts, but they're suddenly swirling like carnivorous insects in my belly.

There are still so many reasons for her to run in the other direction. The comparison of this shitty old shack to her mansion is just too stark to ignore.

She uses two fingers to smooth what must be worry lines on my brow.

"Stop it. Stop worrying. Look at me."

I'm supposed to be in charge right now, but I instantly obey. When I look at her and she lets the light of her love blaze out of her eyes, I take a deep breath and banish all worry-thoughts. How convenient. They're immediately replaced by attraction. No. I take that back, they're replaced by lust.

"You're perfect, Sarah."

I stride to my front door—*our* front door—and practically kick it down in my haste. As I see my living room with fresh eyes and realize what a dump it is, Sarah soothes me again when she says, "Wow, my introduction to your house is *so* much nicer than your introduction to mine. I guarantee it's not going to make me run out of the house to vomit."

What a sweet, thoughtful way to ease my nerves.

CHAPTER THIRTY-EIGHT

When I ease her down, she doesn't give another glance at the shabby furniture or the few dishes scattered on the coffee table. She's a woman on a mission to find the bedroom.

"This place isn't too big. I should be able to find my way."

As she steps away from me, there's something about the way she darts into the hallway that triggers the predator in me.

"Stop!" My lust increases tenfold when she stops immediately at my command. How was I lucky enough to find the other half of my soul?

Standing to my full height, I throw my shoulders back in an intentionally intimidating position. For every step I take toward her, she edges away until her back slams into the wall in the dim, narrow hallway. I muscle closer and slap my palms onto the wall on either side of her head. Her eyes are wide, a little wild. Her gaze follows each of my movements as though her life depends on it as I cage her in.

Her chest rises and falls with quickened breaths that mingle with the charged air between us. "You won't run from me, will you, Sarah?" The dominance in my voice is not just a question but a statement, a claim.

"Never," she whispers, her voice steady despite the flicker of anticipation dancing in her eyes. It pleases me, the instant submission, the way her body leans toward mine, seeking. I can sense the shift in her, the flare of her scent that tells me more than words ever could. She's aroused, the delicate fragrance of her desire unmistakable to an orc's acute senses.

"Good." The word is a low growl, satisfaction curling around the single syllable. My fingers trail down the column of her neck, skirting over her collarbone and ribs to find the hem of her shirt. I take my time, savoring the moment, my touch deliberate as I slip beneath the fabric to trace the soft skin I find there.

Her breath hitches, and I capture her gasp with my mouth, swallowing the sound as our lips meet. It's a dance of power and surrender, and she yields to me beautifully. With careful precision, I peel layers of clothes away from her body, exposing the flushed skin underneath. Each piece that falls to the floor reveals more of her, the smooth curves and valleys that I'm intent on exploring.

Sarah's hands tentatively find their way to my chest, her fingers grazing over the ridges and contours as they seek the hem of my tee. My low growl and intimidating stare put her in her place. A wordless reminder that I'm in charge. I continue unveiling her, the erotic ritual of baring her soul as much as her body.

"Thornn," she breathes out, her voice laced with so much need it sends a jolt of hunger through me.

"Shh," I soothe, even as my hands make quick work of the last barrier to her flesh, her lacy pink panties. "You dressed for this?" I accuse with a smirk.

"Be prepared. It's the Girl Scout motto."

Is she wondering, as I am, what we would both be doing right now if I'd maintained my stupid, stubborn, rigid refusal to reconcile? I let that thought go because thankfully, I was smart enough to see reason.

I gently flick each nipple with my forefinger, then take a step back. It's a wordless pronouncement of ownership that needs no translation. She greets my statement with a gust of her arousal scent, a peek at my eyes, and then a lowered glance.

Standing still in this tight hallway, the only thing moving is my gaze as it roves over her.

"Mine." I expected no answer, no response, but am thrilled when she gives me the slightest, almost imperceptible nod.

I keep her waiting, ramping her fear and arousal as I contemplate which of my thousand fantasies I want to fulfill first.

She begs, "Let me suck you. I've wanted to for so long."

I glare, my eyes flaring wide, a low growl my only answer.

"Please."

CHAPTER THIRTY-EIGHT

"I'm in charge, little human." My words are laced with the power I hold over her. It excites me to remind her of her place, to show her the vast difference in our strengths.

"Then order me to suck you," she counters, her voice dripping with defiance.

A flicker of amusement dances in my eyes, the temptation to laugh at her audacity almost overwhelming. But instead, I maintain my stern demeanor, allowing only a sliver of a smile to touch my lips. "You can't order me to order you to do something, Sarah," I scold, relishing the glimmer of submission in her eyes. "I make the decisions. You follow them."

I outweigh her by a hundred pounds and tower over her, but somehow she finds the nerve to slide gracefully to her knees and look up at me like a starving supplicant wordlessly requesting bread.

How can I say no to the beautiful woman I love, my soulbound, kneeling at my feet?

"Remove my pants. Touch *nothing* without permission." A tiny part in the recesses of my mind wonders if I'm being too harsh, but the thick swirl of her arousal scent greeting my nostrils reminds me why this woman is perfect for me.

"Thank you."

After I toe off my boots, she undoes my button, unzips my jeans, and pulls them down by the waistband, carefully avoiding my cock, which springs toward her so forcefully when it's released I'm surprised it doesn't fling a drop of my pre-cum onto her beautiful face.

Though she's hemmed in against the wall, she manages to press back to get a better look at me. Her gaze is glued to me as she takes me in. Out of the corner of my eye, I see her gripping the waistband of my jeans, which are at thigh height. Her hold is so tight she's white-knuckled. She took my order to touch nothing without permission quite seriously. It's clear she's dying to grip me, explore me. Perhaps it's something in my orc nature that compels me to make her wait.

With her tugging down and me lifting my legs, she manages to pull off my jeans and set them aside. Stepping closer, I swivel my hips, wagging my cock back and forth, painting her lips with my pre-cum. When she eagerly opens her lips to taste me, one guttural warning from the back of my throat is all I need to keep her in line.

"What a good girl you are, Sarah," I praise, a sense of pride welling within me. "Waiting so well." Her small smile lights up her face, and I revel in the power of my words. Needing to keep her on edge, I order, "Look at my face."

The effort she puts into tearing her gaze away from my cock is visible, the intensity of her desire impossible to hide. Her eyes meet mine, hunger burning within them.

Gripping myself at the root, I slide the head of my cock along her lips, praising her with a simple, "Good," when she keeps her mouth closed as I instructed. Her desire fills the air, and I can't help but revel in the intoxicating power I have over her.

There's so much desire pumping through me that I have no lack of pearly pre-cum. I paint one cheek and then the other. Her only response is a stifled gasp and a slight body tremble that shows itself mostly in her hands, which are gripping each other in front of her belly.

"Did you earn the right to suck my cock?" I'm stepping lightly here, wanting her to discover just how much of my dominance she craves, how much of her submission she wants to give me.

"You tell me." Her voice is laced with an uncertainty that sends a shiver down my spine.

"*Fuck,*" I murmur, my cock jerking in eager response. It's as though I chose the sexiest, hottest fantasies from the back of my mind and wrote the script for her.

"Did you think of me every day after you sent me each text?" I push further, wanting her to understand just how much I crave her submission.

"Yes," she breathes, her voice unwavering.

CHAPTER THIRTY-EIGHT

"Did you make yourself come as you thought of me in your bed at night?"

"Yes." That one word is brimming with desire.

"Were some of those thoughts about sucking my cock?"

"*Yes.*" That was a hearty, definitive yes.

"Are you wet right now, thinking about it?"

Her response is immediate, her voice filled with need. "Oh, yes."

Unable to resist a moment longer, I kneel and slide my palm between her legs. Watching her closely for any sign that she's not fully enjoying herself, her response isn't subtle. She opens her knees wider, her pink lips popping open with lust, her gaze glued to my face.

I don't fondle her, don't touch her clit or her entrance, just give her the flat of my palm so gently it's got to make her more desperate than she already is. Instead of pressing against me, which must be her first impulse, she keeps her position and maintains eye contact.

"Such a good girl." Her eyes flutter. "So wet for me. Drenched. Aren't you?"

"Yes," she gasps, her voice filled with desperation.

I reward her with a one-finger swipe from behind her entrance, across the rim, to the side of her clit. Bringing my glistening finger to my lips, I taste her desire as I maintain eye contact. The silence is thick with anticipation as I hold her gaze, savoring the primal connection arcing between us. Her soft, desperate sigh swirls in the silence.

"You may suck my cock." I finally grant her permission, the words a velvet promise of pleasure to come.

I was going to tell her to lick my ball, to gauge her acceptance of what I've considered my shame, but I don't want to push it. Don't want to ruin what we're sharing right now, in case she can't hide her revulsion.

Even though I didn't say the words, she shocks me by dipping low, bypassing the obvious object of her desire, leaning in and licking my sac. There's something about her actions that does more than startle me. It wrecks me somehow.

How many times has this woman told me through words and deeds that I am her soul's desire? I'm who she wants. It doesn't matter that I'm orc and she's human, that I live in this shithole and she owns a mansion, that my body is beaten and far from perfect.

Sarah loves me from the bottom of her heart, from the depths of her soul. In this moment, with more clarity than I've ever possessed, I know that I would go to the ends of the Earth for her. I would die for her.

Right now, though, I'm going to step back into my power and remind her of her submission so that when I finally give her permission to come, she'll scream loud enough that the Goddess herself will hear her all the way to An'Wa.

When I place my palm on her head, I'm reminded with a visceral jolt that my fingers can no longer slide through her silken strands. Her hair is bound in the style mated women in my clan have worn for millennia. She's my mate, my soulbound.

"You make me so proud," I murmur as, with gentle pressure, I guide her mouth to the base of my cock.

I can feel the heat of Sarah's breath against my skin as she inhales deeply, her need palpable in the air around us. The hunger within me intensifies, my senses acutely aware of every detail of this moment. My hands, calloused and rough, glide over her shoulders. Goosebumps rise on her skin as I trail my fingers along the exposed flesh of her throat, a delicious shiver racing through her.

After all those times in Colorado where I slipped away after bringing her to the peaks of pleasure and palmed myself in the bathroom. After all the nights stroking myself in my bed all the while loathing myself for not responding to her texts because I thought I knew what was best for both of us, finally, the woman I love is about to put her lips on me.

CHAPTER THIRTY-NINE

S arah

I've waited for this for so long. Later, when we're not playing this sexy game of dominance and submission, I'll give him his first taste of my sharp tongue as I scold him for making me desperate, making me wait. But for now, I'll bask in the joy of this moment.

Perhaps because he's made me wait so long for this, I take a little delight in delaying his gratification. I simply lean close, open my mouth, and huff hot breaths across his aroused skin. His cock quivers in response. When his hips press closer, my reflexes are good enough that I lean back, as I avoid touching the very thing I've been *aching* to fondle for so long.

"You have a beautiful cock." My voice is soft, breathless. Although my words were whispered, his orc hearing certainly picked them up.

It's a deep emerald green, contrasting with the brighter jade of his skin. The plum-shaped head is almost black in the dim light, standing out against his skin. Thick, pulsing veins trace along the length of his shaft, promising pleasure. And the bead of pre-cum at the tip glistens in the low light, tempting my eyes—and my mouth.

My tongue swipes out to capture the drop before it rolls off the plump head and down the thick shaft. It's salty, potent—a bit like the male himself. Addictive.

Thorn's musky scent hangs heavily in the air, his arousal evident in the earthy and primal fragrance.

I flicker my tongue on the little notch, an inverted V on his crown, exulting in his sharp intake of breath and the way his knees dip, as though the tip of my little human tongue almost cut the legs right out from under him. The big, strong, dominant orc has a weakness? I imagine a dozen ways to exploit it. Later. Now I just want to bring him pleasure.

Resisting the urge to swallow him deep, I choose instead to lick him like a lollipop, all while keeping our gazes locked. I swipe from base to tip over and over, lapping at him, tasting the tang of his salty skin, granting him soft moans of delight when he rewards me with more pearly drops of fluid that leak from his slit.

"I'm not a brute," he says between breathy, masculine pants, "but if you don't get on with it, I might be forced to devise a punishment."

Though I'd thought this was a serious process, a tinkling little laugh escapes me at the thought of Thornn punishing me. I'm not into pain, so it's not the idea of a punishment that amuses me. No, it's the knowledge, down to my very bones, that though he might threaten, this male will never harm me.

As much as I relish his power over me, there's a brat I only this minute discovered who enjoys pushing the envelope—at least with him. Instead of enveloping him in my wet heat—which is what we both desperately want—I ring the ridge of his crown, swirling and licking, then giving it appreciative loud, smacking kisses.

My hands grip his thighs, seeking purchase as he tangles his fingers in my braids. It's a physical embodiment of his growing impatience.

CHAPTER THIRTY-NINE

At last, I take him in one smooth motion as deep as I can. He's huge, filling my mouth, his taste of salt and musk coating my tongue. He's using all his self-control not to press farther than I want, allowing me to set the limits.

I use all my skills to provide him bliss, my palms circling his base, one on top of the other. Then I use my hands and mouth to give him all the ecstasy I can provide. He rewards me with a hiss of pleasure as his hips buck. With my head bobbing and my hands twisting, I'm perfectly attuned to the male I love.

"So good. So good to me, Sarah."

His praises are like gold coins, showering me in riches. I numbly wonder if I could live on his softly whispered words alone.

"Sarah!" The sound is sharp, a warning. Does he think I want to pull off him, let him spill himself anywhere but on my desperate tongue? I've waited *months* for this.

I suck, my cheeks hollowing as I hum my pleasure and find a way to take him deeper inside me. My palms twist on his shaft, working in tandem to bring him to the edge. Perhaps I have a little sadist living inside me, because I make him hover here for a moment, building him even higher before I suck harder, bob faster, and make him spiral into bliss.

"Fuck!" He shouts as he spills down my throat, giving me a sense of triumph. I made this big, strong, otherworldly orc lose himself. He pulses against my tongue, his hips pistoning. Growls escape his mouth as he grips my scalp so tightly I feel the bite. It thrills me to know I've made him lose control, forced him to a place where there's no room for worries. I doubt he allows himself to visit that peaceful feeling very often.

Placing his forearms on the wall, he sags against it as though he doesn't have the strength to stand. He's huffing as though he just ran a race while I lick him clean. He's muttering in orcish. Is it a prayer to the Goddess he loves so much, or praise for me? Perhaps a combination of both.

He must have gotten his second wind, because he stands tall, leans to lift me from under my armpits, then strides, carrying me down the hallway to his bedroom.

"I'm going to kiss you and stroke every inch of your naughty, naughty body and then I'm going to dive into you, Sarah. I'm going to make you scream my name. I should have done this months ago."

Though I want to say, "Whose fault was that?" I bite back my retort. I love him too much, and now he's my mate.

CHAPTER FORTY

T hornn

Later, I'll finish chastising myself for denying myself the bliss of her mouth on me for *months*. My lack of a ball was of zero importance to her, and I let it drive me crazy—drive us both crazy—as well as keep us apart. I let that go, though, and focus on the beautiful female in my arms.

After setting her at the foot of my bed, facing it, I say, "Don't move!" with all the force I can muster without raising my voice.

I'm going to arouse her as slowly and methodically as she did me. Pressing myself against her back so not a speck of air is between us, I wordlessly remind the primitive part of her brain how big I am, that I'm taller than her, full of unrelenting muscle. This should show her, on a visceral level, that I'm in charge.

Tugging her braid, I arch her neck and expose the vulnerable column of her throat, keeping our gazes locked in that unsettling position.

"You're mine," I rasp, my statement brooking no argument, although I know she won't give me any.

I wonder if those two words mean the same to her as they do to me. Do they remind her that I'm in charge? That I can move her body in any position, any way that pleases me? That I can touch her wherever and whenever I want?

Perhaps those words were eloquent enough to communicate all of that. They surely made her arousal scent billow from between her legs.

Is she thinking the same thing as I am now? That I can edge her for hours? Until she whimpers? Begs? Until she wonders if death would be less painful than waiting on the razor's edge for release, as she's denied the privilege of falling into the abyss of ecstasy?

Though it's been mere minutes since I spilled down her perfect throat, my cock is already swollen with need. I grind my hips, my cock pulsing against her back, beginning the tease. It's a reminder of what I have, of what she wants.

Leaning over her, I mouth along the hard line of her jaw, lick the tendon on her throat, and nip her collarbone until she sags against me. Then I step away until our only physical connection is my grip on her hips. I let her sway on her feet, wondering where my sturdy heat went, why I left her alone.

Easing close again, I breathe a gust of warm air from her nape down her spine to the crack between her cheeks, then watch as goosebumps sizzle along the same path. I've barely touched her, yet she's panting. Peeking over her shoulder, I see her pretty brown nipples bead in the cool night air.

"What do you want?" I'm an asshole. Don't deserve her. I just used my most concerned, sympathetic voice, letting her believe I'll grant her what she asks for, all while knowing I have absolutely no intention of fulfilling her request. At least not right this minute.

"I want whatever you want." Her answer is breathless.

Perfect. How did I get so lucky? It *almost* makes me want to skip to the finish line and glove myself inside her wet heat right this moment. Almost.

Instead, I trace my tusks down her spine, one on each side of her vertebrae. It doesn't escape my notice that I wouldn't have these two tusks without Sarah, without her generosity, her affection.

CHAPTER FORTY

My tusk points aren't sharp, but they're not particularly blunted either. It wakes her up from her dreamy daze, making her stand straighter and crane to look at me over her shoulder.

"I'm not human," I murmur, as though she needed a reminder.

I graze my calloused hands over her shoulders, then slide my huge palms down her arms and along the outside of her thighs. It's a thing of beauty, seeing my jade skin against hers, so creamy and soft.

Perhaps it's a factor of my blood, my very DNA, but I want to take her from behind. To pound into her, maybe biting her shoulder as I do. Orc females fight back. At the beginning of a relationship, dominance must be established, often with wrestling or physical fights.

With Sarah and me, dominance has already been established. I've found that my beautiful new mate wants nothing more than to give me exactly what I want. Perhaps that's why I don't want to surge into her from behind, as my primitive brain is demanding.

Tonight, I want to gaze into her eyes, to see the expression on her face when I slide into her for the first time, when I claim her.

"Tell me what you want. And don't say 'whatever you want.'"

"I want your mouth on mine." She didn't stop to think, which tells me she's been yearning for this for a long time. "I want your amber gaze on mine. I want to hear your words—whether they're in orcish or English, I don't care."

I told her to stand perfectly still. Perhaps that's why her hands are moving behind her in slow motion as they reach for me. She's bucking my order. She must be desperate to feel my skin, my heat.

"I want our bodies to fit together perfectly, as I know they will. I want your brute strength and your profound tenderness. I want to feel all the love you have for me, that you've hidden from yourself and me for the last one hundred days. I want your seed in me, Thornn. I want to love you forever."

"You shall have all of that, my Sarah, because you are the other half of my soul."

I lift her with every ounce of tenderness I possess and place her on the bedspread as though she's a priceless treasure. Our breath mingles as we kiss, just as she requested.

The warmth of her breath grazes against my skin, electric sparks sizzling down my spine. Her soft tongue brushes against my bottom lip, teasingly asking for entry, and I part my lips to let her in.

Our tongues tangle, exploring each other's mouths with a curiosity that speaks volumes about our newfound expression of love. The taste of her mouth is intoxicating—sweet like honey with a hint of fruit... strawberry?

She gently wraps her hands around my neck and pulls me closer, pressing herself against me with a passion that matches my own. I groan softly at the contact, feeling her breasts flatten against my chest. It sends a jolt of desire shooting through my system as I return the embrace with fervor, one hand sliding slowly down her back while the other tenderly cups her face.

Her breath hitches as our tongues play together. Her heart pounds against my chest, declaring the extent of her arousal. My teeth scrape gently across her lower lip, and a soft moan escapes her throat as we dive deeper into the kiss, our lips moving hungrily. Neither of us can get enough.

Her hands slide down my chest, tracing the ridges of my muscles before gliding through the furrows of the hair she just braided. She tugs one of my braids, teasing me, and I chuckle against her mouth.

The bed squeaks slightly as, in sync, we scoot closer together, our bodies pressed tightly from chest to thighs. The heat between us is palpable.

After tracing her tongue along the outline of my ear, she whispers, "Have I ever told you how sexy these are? One of the traits that marks you as different? As Other? As special?"

Only this female could remind me of my Otherness in such a loving way. She tips her head so I can see her lazy smile, then dips lower to nibble at a spot behind my ear. She scrapes harder than I would have expected until her tongue laps at the spot she just bit. Her fingers dig into my skin, her nails raking softly, and it only serves to fuel my passion further.

We break the kiss for a moment to catch our breath, our bodies still pressed together like two pieces of a puzzle that finally fit. I look down at her, taking in every inch of her perfect human form—those breasts that jiggle enticingly with every breath she takes, the inviting curve of her hip, the mischievous sparkle in her blue eyes.

"*Amnoch baleen mayore*, my love. *Krenash ja f'ren*." She asked for my words. I will give them to her. "I belong to you, my love. Forever and always."

I straddle her, then lean to her breasts, sucking, nipping, and stabbing her little nipple with the point of my tongue, which I learned in Colorado drives her mad with desire. She scissors her legs, fighting against my bulk until her legs open, offering me the cradle between her thighs.

"I love you," I tell her with all the sincerity I possess. It's surprising how easily those words slip from my lips after keeping them inside all this time.

"Have you tortured me enough, love?" She manages to scold me and adore me with the same words.

My gaze flares red, obscuring everything at the edges of my vision until all I see is her—my soulbound, my forever-mate. As I slide my cock between her slippery folds, I ensure our gazes are connected and press into her. My cock is so thick and long, I wondered if I could breach her without pain.

She grips my shoulders and spears me with the sweetest smile as I ease my way in.

"I knew we'd fit perfectly, Thornn."

Watching her face for any indication of discomfort, I keep going as I rock in and ease out, going farther with each thrust until I'm fully seated inside her wet, welcoming heat.

I assume it's Sarah who is trembling until I realize it's me. My hands gripping her hips are vibrating. My emotions are overwhelming. Instead of feeling vulnerable because of the depth of my love for her, I allow myself to swim in it, to relish it. This is more than I'd ever allowed myself to hope for.

When Sarah's eyes shutter closed and she thrusts her pelvis toward me, a silent request for more, I realize the time for soft emotions is over. I need to give my female all the pleasure I've denied her for so long.

I surge into her, adjusting my angle until her lids fly wide and she gasps with pleasure. That's the spot. Lifting her leg to place her sole on my pec, I open her even wider to slide in even deeper.

Increasing my rhythm, we move together as though we've performed this intimate dance a hundred times. My hips thrust faster, harder, and she meets me stroke for stroke. Our skin slaps together, the sound echoing through the room.

The mattress groans under our weight as we grind against each other, the springs creaking in ecstasy beneath us. Each thrust forces a gasp from her lips, each moan rumbles against my chest. Her soft hands trail up my back, fingers digging into the muscles there as she arches into me with a feral cry.

When I bite and nip at her neck, she bares the tender column more fully to me. My pride and arousal surges at her acceptance of me, of everything I am. My cock pulses inside her, as I find her sweet spot over and over again, making her gasp and moan as we both lose ourselves in this primal dance.

We breathe heavily, our hearts pounding in unison. Her nails scrape my back and I let out a low, guttural groan, instinctively pressing harder into her, seeking release. She meets my every move with the same ferocity, her body arching to meet mine.

As I thrust deeper, pressure builds at the base of my spine. I bite down on my lower lip to stifle a growl of pleasure. Sarah moans against my neck, her body tensing beneath mine as she comes undone with a wordless cry.

Her hot walls clench around my cock, pushing me closer to my limit. With one last hard thrust, I give in to primitive urgency and allow my release. My seed pulses in time with my shouted roars of ecstasy.

Watching her lovely face, now bathed in the red glow, squeeze in ecstasy as she shouts her pleasure, I can see the moment the soulbond captures her. In our teens, we were told only orcs experienced soulbinding, and even among our people it was rare. But all the orc/human couples in the Zone have soulbonds. I'm not surprised to see it on her flushed, surprised face.

I resist the urge to fall to the bed in a heap of sated pleasure. Instead, I put my weight on my forearms, bracketing her head. Our faces are only an inch apart as I feel her hot panting exhales graze over my face.

It's obvious how much effort it takes for her to force her lids open, but she does so to gaze at me. My heart clenches with the force of her love. It's tall as a sequoia and forceful as a tidal wave.

Hearing her tell me how much she loves me is wonderful, mending places deep within me that have needed healing for so long. But there's something about the strength of this penetrating gaze that burrows even deeper than my beating heart. It arrows to my very soul, filling me up, repairing the cracks inside me, making me feel whole again.

This awareness steals some of my strength, so I relent to the urge to fall to my side on the mattress, yet I bring her with me. We're still connected. I don't ever want to leave the warmth of her welcoming channel.

"We're soulbound, my love. Can you feel it? Our connection? Stronger than it was before we came? Endless? More than you could have imagined only moments ago?"

The woman who just shouted my name in passion and came so hard I'm sure the thick hide of my shoulders is bleeding, now looks shy.

"Emma told me about the bond, but I thought it was presumptuous to expect it. This is it, Thornn?" She closes her eyes and breathes deeply. "It's more powerful than I dared hope for."

My purr thrums stronger than ever as I nuzzle my nose to her neck, thrilling at the scent of her that now proclaims she's mine to the very heart and soul of her.

I trail the pad of my finger down her cheek so gently I wonder if she would even feel it if her eyes were closed. "My love, you own me. All of me. Every inch. Now and forever."

CHAPTER FORTY-ONE

Sarah

The only thing that tells me whether it's day or night is the sun streaming through Thornn's bedroom window. I lost all sense of time. Does that male have no refractory period whatsoever? We made love and dozed and made love again all through the night. It was wonderful and intimate and, at times, overwhelming.

Although our first time was all I'd hoped it would be and *more*, filled with love and passion and amazing pleasure, the rest of the night was filled with all the promise of our new relationship.

I have to give Thornn credit; he made no secret about his dominant side. He never tried to hide it, so it was no surprise when, on our third or fourth time last night, he let his orc genetics have free rein. There's something about him ordering me around, edging me until I beg, that fulfills something deep within me that yearns to submit.

Although I imagine there will be more of that later today, right now I'm famished. Good thing I smell food.

"You up yet, sleepyhead?" he calls from another room. "I didn't realize you'd be such a lightweight. Next time I'll have to go easier on you."

He eases the door open with his hip and steps in with a tray laden with bacon and eggs and toast.

"Sorry, no bagels. Now that you're here..." He stops like a wind-up toy that runs out of energy. The expression on his face is... is that awe? As though he can't believe I'm really here, in his bed, looking at him as though I can't wait for him to join me so I can cover his face with kisses?

He shakes his head, his thoughts coming back online, and finishes his sentence. "Now that you're here, I'll keep the kitchen stocked with all your favorite things."

"I only have one favorite thing I can't do without." I toss him a brazen look and pat the bed next to me. "You."

He straightens the bed as well as he can, considering not one of the four corners of the fitted sheet managed to keep its hold on the mattress during the onslaught of passion we shared, as well as that I'm still lying in the middle of it. He hands me a cup of coffee and sets plates in a line down in the middle of the bed.

His careful work almost dumps over when his considerable weight dips the bed in his direction. When I start to dig in, he shakes his head and eases my fork from my hand.

"I'm your mate. I'll feed you, take care of you." He gets the sweetest, almost bashful look as he whispers to himself, "My soulbound," with shocked pride.

Breakfast is a slow affair of him selecting the perfect bites of bacon and eggs, sometimes in tandem, sometimes alone. At times, he places them on toast for a special treat, then gives me a moment for a sip of coffee.

"I could get used to this." I realize this is honeymoon behavior. Things like this don't last.

"Good, because a good orc mate will feed his female like this often. It's one of the ways we show our affection."

Hiding my surprise, I commend myself for my excellent taste in mates.

CHAPTER FORTY-ONE

"You know all those days I wrote you a text a day?"

"Mmm." I've changed the tone between us. He's wary now, so I'd better explain quickly.

"When I wasn't texting you or working on my dissertation, I was planning for the future I wanted."

"Ohh?"

"I guess I should tell you what that future looks like in my head."

He stacks the plates, sets them on his nightstand, and lies back down, placing his head on his palm, letting me know he's all ears.

"I'm a realist. My condo won't be safe for us, not until the world changes." A cloud shadows his expression and his gaze darts from mine. The look of guilt on his face makes me reach out to skim my fingers along his cheek.

"Like I said, I'm a realist." I scoot closer and grab his free hand in mine, lacing our fingers. "So I figured I'd end up living with you in the Zone."

The cloud on his face turns thunderous. "I don't want you here, Sarah. The Zone is a pit."

"I can't argue with you, but I visit often enough to know it's a pit in an unsavory part of town filled with wonderful people and a lot of love. I'm going to do fine here." He scowls. "No. Not fine. Thornn, I'm going to *thrive*."

He perks up. Perhaps it was the vehemence in my last statement that helped him believe me.

"So it was a happy accident that you lost your apartment and got this shitty little bungalow. When I sell my condo, we're going to make this a little palace."

I can see his mind working, can almost smell the gears grinding.

"Since I moved in, I've thought of dozens of ways to improve this place, Sarah. I just knew I'd never have the money." His thumb circles the center of my palm.

"Not only will we improve it, but we'll draw up plans to *expand*... when the time is right." My eyebrow flash hopefully tells him all he needs to know about what would necessitate said expansion.

"Orclings, Sarah? Really?" He's beaming.

Perhaps it's the memory of just how gleeful he was as he edged me mercilessly in the middle of the night that makes me taunt, "Of course. Emma and Kam's child will need a friend. I had to scrape up a father somewhere."

He lurches to straddle me, hold me down, and rasp the edges of his tusks against my chest.

"Just for that, I'll have to hold you hostage in this bed until I can think of ways to retaliate," he threatens with a soft smile.

We exchange sloppy kisses amidst happy giggles until I pull back.

"Give me a second to finish telling you my vision of the future. Then, big guy, you can retaliate all you want. I'm learning to like your little punishments."

After one sweet, warm kiss to my lips, he gives me his I'm-all-ears look. Adorable.

"At the condo..." I notice it's already second nature not to call the condo home anymore. *Here* is my home. With Thornn. "I've printed out a map and marked all the isolated rest stops between here and Verdant Park. We'll bring a gas can, so we don't have to stop at any gas stations that aren't large, well-lit, and safe."

His head is cocked. He's still listening although his lips are pursed, skeptical.

"I picture us filling the car with food, snacks, drinks, and an extra gas can and making the trip to the mansion every December. We'll decorate and get kerosene heaters for the back porch so we can make love on the round bed where we fell in love. Just the two of us."

CHAPTER FORTY-ONE

He looks dreamy for a moment, then his handsome face falls. "What about your job, Sarah? All the work you did to get your doctorate. You can't give that up to live here." He gestures around the room.

"One day, when you let me out of this bed, I'll introduce you to the Internet. People use it for the most interesting things these days. Many use it to gather information. I'll use it to teach. Distance learning. It gets more popular every year."

I reach to smooth the two worry lines etched between his eyebrows.

"Life is going to be amazing. Remind me later to tell you what I want to do with the pitiful park where you proposed last night. Now, I believe you promised me a punishment."

CHAPTER FORTY-TWO: EPILOGUE

Thornn

To think that this was born the night we reconciled a little over a year ago. While I was busy being besotted, my guts twisting in knots, at war with itself—fighting between desiring her more than breath itself, yet wanting to keep her safe—she was vowing to make monumental changes to her adopted world.

We had our little stay-moon, which is what she called the honeymoon we took in my bungalow when we didn't leave the place for a week as we made love all day except for food and sleep.

She went a whole day without looking at her email, and lo and behold, that was the day she received word that her committee approved her dissertation. The moment we came up for air from our marathon sex, we had our friends over for an impromptu celebration. Every single one of them called her Dr. Hillman at least three times—she never tired of hearing it.

To her credit, she was great meeting all the huge orcs from the fire station as well as all my other friends from the Zone. She was especially taken by one of the youngest firefighters, Durga.

CHAPTER FORTY-TWO: EPILOGUE

"He's just such an odd combination of fearless firefighter and gentle soul. He's going to make some lucky woman very happy."

The amount of nagas, minotaurs, wolven, and more that we managed to cram into our little bungalow was mind-boggling.

After that party, when Sarah wasn't busy sending resumes to every college in the U.S. with a distance learning program, she began working to improve the park.

"How could the local government allow such a travesty? It's almost a full city block, yet there's little more than two ancient picnic tables and an antique swing set," she'd railed. "Pathetic!"

She proceeded to use her newfound passion to meet just about everyone in the Zone. After pumping the elders about what it was like on An'Wa, she invited everyone to town hall meetings where she showed endless pictures of trees, shrubs, and plants. With input from my people, she accumulated a list of foliage that looked most like what people would have found in our home place.

Over the last year, she lobbied the government for approval to make changes as well as asking for funds to make her vision happen. When the government offered a fraction of what it would take to make the improvements, she forked over the rest of the money herself.

"Aunt Beth would approve," she'd told me with conviction. "What else am I going to do with all the money from the sale of those bearer bonds and jewelry we worked so hard for?"

So, over a year later, here we are at the Grand Opening of An'Wa Gardens Park. It's hard to remember the barren wasteland it was that night when we reunited. Although I was born on Earth, the elders tell us this is as close to An'Wa as they've been in over a quarter of a century.

The park is lush and filled with trees. Children's play equipment is dotted along a dappled trail. In the center is a huge firepit ringed by thick logs. The elders assure us, this is how the clans would arrange things for their meetings.

On An'Wa, all the clans lived separately. I think this is an improvement. Here, clan divisions have slipped away. Orcs, minotaur, wolven, and the like all gather together, one family united. I'm proud to live in the Zone, as is my lovely mate, my Sarah.

"When was the last time you sat down, love?"

"Umm?"

"Don't give me that innocent look." I lift her in my arms. Despite her pregnant belly, it's just as easy as it's ever been.

After striding to one of the new picnic tables, I set her down gently.

Maybe she sees a faraway, wistful look on my face, because she asks, "Thinking about our mating night?"

"You know me well. It's hard to sit at a picnic table in this park and not think about the night I almost lost you."

"It was also the night you found me, big guy. The night I braided your hair because you felt whole again. The night you braided mine so every man, woman, and child in the Zone would know who I belong to."

"Mine." The word slips out. I usually only make the statement in the bedroom. It never ceases to ramp her arousal. But it pops into my head at other times of the day.

I'll be doing my job and thinking of her, or cooking her favorite foods, or simply when I come home from work to find her grading papers on her computer. Then the thought will arrow into my brain with the oddest combination of love and lust and possession. *Mine.* That one word says it all.

"Time for you to say a few words." I reach out to help her make the difficult transition from sitting to standing. "You've been a blessing to this community, to my people."

"They're my people too, now. Our orclings will belong here, will be raised here, will visit their grandparents in this park."

CHAPTER FORTY-TWO: EPILOGUE

I'm so glad she and her parents repaired their relationship. They may never be thrilled with her choice of mates, but they are cordial, which is all I require.

As we walk to the crowd waiting at the firepit, I thank the Goddess for bringing Sarah into my life.

"You're the best thing that ever happened to me," I say as I pull her into my arms.

"Yeah?"

"No contest. Hands down. The. Very. Best. Thing." I give her little kisses with each word, then gently cover her small hand with my large one as she strokes her belly.

"I don't know, my love. The best things may be yet to come."

DEAR READER

If you haven't figured it out yet, I love a damaged hero! It's so much fun matching them with the perfect human mate so they can fully heal! I hope you found Thornn and Sarah's romance fun and spicy.

Next up? Durga's story (I gave him a little mention in the epilogue). Keep reading for a Sneak Peek of his novel.

I've got so many freebies for you! Go to alanakhan.com

Hugs,

Alana

SNEAK PEEK: EMBER'S SPARK

In a world divided by barbed-wire fences, their love defies all boundaries, igniting a passion that sets their worlds on fire.

Raisa

From the moment he saw me, the handsome orc went into protection mode, even though I insisted I didn't need his help. His piercing gaze and commanding touch awakened desires I never knew I possessed. And that long, black tongue? Well, let's just say it defies the laws of physics.

In his arms, I find solace, shelter, and a love that's thrilling yet forbidden. But as danger lurks in the shadows, I'm forced to confront a choice: safety or a love that sets my soul ablaze?

Durga

Raisa's combination of fierce independence and vulnerability ignites an attraction that leaves me breathless and hungry for more. Although our love is taboo, I'll battle man and orc alike to keep her safe.

Though our love defies the odds, together we're unstoppable.

Buy on Amazon.com/FREE in KU or get the audiobook for only $5.99 on my Alanaverse store: shopalanakhan.com

Chapter One

Durga

This hole in the fence has been here for years, but it's only lately I've begun sneaking out of the Integration Zone.

Though I was born elsewhere, Earth is the only home I've ever known. I was two when a hole ripped through the sky on An'Wa. I can't remember it, but I've heard the story so many times that the pictures in my mind are so vivid it's hard to believe the memories aren't my own.

Although it's been twenty-five years, my people still talk about it as though it happened yesterday. Many species, many clans met at the twice-yearly Gathering. There was music, trading, eating, and drinking.

On the second night of the festivities, the skies opened up, lightning continuously lit the sky and thunder rolled for long minutes.

A black hole appeared in the sky and silver threads, strong as steel, reached through the hole, wrapped around random people, and sucked them through to Earth.

Five thousand of us landed in the Mojave Desert, including my mother and me. They called us Others and placed us here in the Integration Zone, a fenced area on the outskirts of Los Angeles. We languished for years until recently when they finally allowed us outside the gates.

Allowed is one thing. Welcomed is quite another. I'm taking my life in my hands by sneaking through this hidden gap in the fence.

On An'Wa we were warriors when necessary, nomadic in our very essence. At least the orc clans were. Perhaps the need to roam is in my blood. Or maybe it's that my entire life has been restricted to ten square city blocks. Now that I can leave, it's against my nature to stay confined.

I unroll the barbed wire from where it's made to look like a seamless part of the fence. After crawling out, I roll it back. Although I'm only inches away from the Zone, I feel different already. At least it's a *taste* of freedom. Somehow, it's easier to smell autumn in the air out here.

It's easy to know where to go. I follow my nose to the water. We're far from the ocean. Ghettos aren't in places with prime views. There's a run-down park I discovered nearby. It has trees and a small lake. There's a children's playground there.

Some do-gooders donated play equipment to the Zone when I was still young enough to enjoy it, but twirling on a little metal roundy-round inside a fenced prison probably feels far different from how humans feel twirling while breathing free.

I avoid the illuminated puddles cast by the streetlights, making my way in looping patterns to stay on the darkened parts of the street. I'm a head taller than most human men and far bulkier. It's not easy to be stealthy because of my size, but my genetics help me walk silently.

I've seen pictures drawn by elders who remember An'Wa, but I can't picture the forests as clearly as I'd like. Still, I imagine my father and members of my clan stalking game, hunting with bows and arrows, breathing air that was somehow fresher than here, and enjoying the brilliance provided by two suns.

The scent of water is closer, pulling me off the street, through autumn-colored, golden-leafed trees, and into the park. It's a small place, pitiful compared to what I see on TV, but it feeds my soul somehow.

Shit! I was so deep in my thoughts, so entranced by the smell of fresh water, that I didn't catch her scent on the air.

It's two in the fucking morning. What is a little girl doing out at this time of night?

She's on a swing, one leg tucked under her and one on the ground. Her hands clutch the metal chains as she stares off into space. She smells worried. Has she run away from home? Been kicked out by abusive parents?

I'm at the edge of the trees, a step away from the open playground. Just as I'm about to retreat into the shadows, she sees me. I know she couldn't have heard me. I didn't snap a twig or crush a dried leaf.

For whatever reason, her gaze arrowed to me. The only humans I've been around are the teachers and authorities who come to the Zone for work. I've never been around a child before.

Look at her eyes—wide and terrified. Her mouth is an open O. I put my hands up, palms out, the wordless statement that I mean no harm. As I back up, ready to turn and hurry back to the Zone, I hear her softly spoken words, "Don't go."

Chapter Two

Raisa

I was raised six blocks from here and as an adult, I still live nearby. Even though we're close to the Zone, I was never allowed to walk near there as a kid and haven't explored it as an adult. I've seen pictures of the Others, though, and even in the dim moonlight, with him mostly hidden in the trees, there's no mistaking he's an orc.

I come here at night to think, or when I can't sleep, or both—like tonight. Despite being in a shitty part of town, I've never had a problem here. I'm not stupid. I have pepper spray and an eight-inch kitchen knife in my backpack.

Although he's dwarfed by the trees, it's clear he's bigger than any man I've ever known. Not just tall, but built like a linebacker—a *big* linebacker. It's hard to see his features, but they have the hard lines and angles of his species.

Even in the dim light, his dark brown hair is lustrous and pulled back in braids. Beaded necklaces adorn his naked chest, and tribal tats cover both arms. Fear lances through me when moonlight glints off his long, ivory tusks.

He rears his head and begins his retreat. By the amount of whites showing around his irises, I wonder if he's more frightened of me than I am of him.

"Don't go!" The words are out of my mouth before I think them through.

It's two in the morning. I'm a denizen of the night and come here often to think. Tonight, it's money and rent and the hella-expensive software I need but can't afford.

I seldom encounter people here, other than couples who do their hurried business in a little plastic culvert meant for kids to play in, but used at night for drug deals and furtive sex. Who was the genius who thought that was the perfect thing to put on a kids' playground?

No one is there now. It's just me and the orc, who looks unsure as he makes a "who, me?" gesture when I tell him not to go. When I wave him over a second time, he eases forward, edging toward me sideways as if he's trying to make himself a smaller target. I can't stifle a quiet scoff as I think he seems more fearful of me than I am of him.

I pull my little backpack off the ground and place it on my lap. If I need the pepper spray or the knife, all I need to do is pull them from the outer pouch.

"Are you lost?" His voice is so deep it seems to seep inside my skin and rumble through me. "Running away from your parents? I can walk you home or," he gulps nervously, "get you to the police."

"You think I'm a child?"

His head tilts. I've stumped him, which means he definitely thinks I'm a kid.

"I'm a grown woman. Not in need of saving." Although how sweet that rescuing a child in distress was his first thought.

"Never seen a human child in person. You just seem so… small, and," he gestures around him, "you're on a swing."

Suddenly, I want to know more about this man—this orc—who's never seen a human child.

Why have I never researched much about the Zone when it's only a few blocks away? I want to rectify that and this seems like the perfect opportunity.

I'm not sure which of us is in the most danger. A five-foot-nothing female in a shady part of town, or a humongous orc who most humans would agree has no business outside the Zone at this time of night.

"I come here when I can't sleep."

He nods in understanding. "I come here to... breathe."

He's seen so few humans, he had no idea of my age. I could say much the same about my lack of knowledge of Others. This male might be eighteen or thirty-five for all I know. Suddenly I'm filled with questions.

"Have a seat. I won't bite." I take a good look at his ivory tusks as they flash in the moonlight and chuckle at my inadvertent joke.

It's only when he eases onto the swing next to me and the chains creak under his weight that I realize how massive this male is. It's awkward conversing on swings in the first place since they all face the same direction. But to look at his face, I not only have to twist in my seat, but the back of my head almost rests on my shoulder.

I jump off and get back on the swing, facing the opposite direction, making it easier to converse.

"You're so tiny." His chin is tipped almost to his chest so he can look at me.

"Maybe it's not that I'm so tiny. Maybe it's that you're so big."

We laugh. It breaks the ice.

Perhaps it's that we're on a children's playground and my serious mood has vanished, but I place my hand toward him in a high-five position. He immediately responds, placing his palm against mine.

We're both fascinated by our size difference as our palms meet. I can't hold back an astonished giggle as my doll-sized hand rests against his, which is almost the size of a dinner plate. When our palms are laid flat against each other, the tips of my fingers barely make it past his palm.

Just like that, we start a conversation. No. Conversation doesn't describe what happens between us.

A conversation implies social niceties, little verbal games people play as we dance around platitudes and white lies and generalities and deceptions.

What this orc and I do is dive deep into a baring of souls.

Perhaps that's because we both assume we live in different worlds, that we'll never see each other again. There's something safe about telling my private thoughts to this gentle giant, this male whose first thought upon meeting me was that he had to save me somehow.

After just a few interchanges, I jump into the deep end. I tell him how odd it was having a white mom, yet growing up not knowing what bubble to fill in when it asked for my race, and how I begged her to just tell me who my father was.

She only answered with lies. It was only a few years ago she admitted she didn't know who my father was because there were several choices. And by several, I think she meant many.

He shared how it felt to be an outsider his whole life and how hard it was to lose his mother a few years ago. My heart pangs with sympathy and guilt. Was I really moaning about my circumstances to a male who isn't even supposed to be on this planet? An orc straight out of a fairytale who's been fenced inside the Zone his whole life?

"Sorry. I was insensitive."

He shrugs as though he has no idea why I'm apologizing.

As we talk and I spill thoughts and emotions I've never shared with a soul, I find myself forgetting about our differences and paying attention to our similarities.

And then I notice how handsome he is. The Others are hidden away and rarely mentioned except by the Purists with their ubiquitous rhetoric about how the "abominations" don't belong on Earth and should be exterminated.

This explains why I've seen few pictures of orcs. Unlike the rugged and fearsome appearance of the single picture in my history book, this male is a breathtaking masterpiece who could rival a divine being.

At first glance, my eyes are drawn to his powerful brow, sculpted like ancient stone cliffs, with a subtle arch that frames his eyes with regal elegance. Beneath that prominent brow, a pair of mesmerizing amber eyes gleam like rare gemstones, capturing the essence of both earth and fire.

His strong, chiseled cheekbones suggest a warrior's prowess with a hint of refinement. Maybe it's his eyes, or maybe the way he stood at the edge of the trees, ready to retreat at my request that imbues him with a touch of vulnerability, as if he bears the weight of the world on his shoulders.

Beneath his distinguished nose is a generous mouth, made more interesting by the way it easily works around those brutish tusks.

The way his braids are pulled back accentuates his pointed, yet oddly graceful, orcish ears. Top of Form

I forgot I'd read that orcs' tongues were black, but when I catch a glimpse of it in the watery moonlight, my thoughts become fixated on what it would feel like pressing between my lips. A moment later, I wonder what it would feel like exploring between my legs.

"When the laws changed, allowing us to have jobs, to police ourselves inside the Zone, to work at our own firehouse, I jumped at the chance to be a firefighter. I felt like it was what I was meant to—"

It's only when he stops mid-sentence, eyes wide, that I realize I was barely listening. I'd been wondering what his tusks would feel like against my tender skin if he ate me out.

"What are you thinking?" This isn't the tone he's been using since we met, hushed, like you'd speak to a frightened child. This is a demand.

We've been talking for what, an hour? Two? I haven't heard this timbre in his voice before. It's an octave lower.

"Hmm?"

A different person, perhaps a person I'd been having a *conversation* with instead of vomiting out the deepest secrets of my soul, would say nothing to my pretend-innocent question. This male, whose name I don't know because we skipped the surface pleasantries, says, "Orcs' sense of smell is ten times more acute than humans. You're thinking about sex."

Busted. So fucking busted.

Fuck the baring of souls. I want to run home. I don't want to admit I was thinking about him eating me out. Shit! Does *thinking* the words "eating me out" intensify my scent?

I want to act offended and challenge his observation. To jump off my swing and snatch my bag off the ground where I let it drop an hour ago when I realized I didn't need my knife. But running away without a word would dishonor the amazing talk we've been having. I can't do that.

"Hey, I should probably go." I slide to my feet and grip my bag as though it will shield his nose from my horny pheromones.

Right now, he should rise, pretend he didn't mention my scent, and say goodnight.

"I shouldn't have said that. Even though I grew up on Earth, I've never really talked to a human before, not one my age. I thought this was how it's done. Honesty, you know?"

He's apologizing. It's sincere. Yet the words slap me because he's right. *Honesty, you know?* Yeah, we were doing that, weren't we? Until I got scared.

"Don't apologize. I'm not used to anyone knowing when I'm... and then when you mentioned it..." I wave my hand randomly, hoping I made my point.

Chapter Three

Durga

She's standing, I'm sitting. I can see why I thought she was a child. She's tiny. But clearly a woman. If her generous breasts and a nipped waist that swells to rounded hips didn't give her away, her scent certainly does.

"I made you uncomfortable. Things are different inside the fence."

"You..." She was going to say something, but her words drop off, forgotten.

Her black eyes glitter in the moonlight as she seems to get lost in my gaze. Her arousal scent swirls around us, but I like the smell underneath it, the slightly citrusy smell of her skin and her breath.

As she leans in closer, her lips just inches from mine, I feel the warmth radiating from her body. The soft moonlight bathes us in its glow, casting a spell that only deepens the intimacy we created when we shared our thoughts.

Her eyes meet mine, their intensity mirroring the wild beating of my own heart. We're both suspended in time, oblivious to the world around us. The playground has been neutral ground, a world where our differences don't matter.

With a slight tremor in her voice, she whispers, "Kiss me."

Despite her scent, I didn't expect this. Part of me wants to persuade her she shouldn't do this. There are only a few human-Other relationships on the planet. It's simply not done.

But I don't say a thing. Instead, I taste the anticipation in the air. It's a heady mix of desire and uncertainty, blending with the sharp tang of metal from the playground equipment. As her breath mingles with mine the sweetness of her citrus scent seduces my senses.

Leaning forward, I close the distance between us. Our lips meet in a featherlight touch, an exploration of the unknown. The sensation is electrifying, as if an invisible current surges through our bodies, creating a connection that defies logic or reason.

As our kiss deepens, her fingertips graze my cheek, sending shivers down my spine, while my hands instinctively grip her waist to pull her closer.

The taste of her lips is intoxicating, a fusion of sweetness and sparks. My fingers slide through her glossy, black hair as I press deeper, sliding my tongue along the seam of her lips.

I wasn't sure she would open herself to me. A moment ago, she looked ready to run, like a prey animal. But her tiny hands grip my biceps, then tighten as though she doesn't want this kiss to end.

Opening my thighs, I slip a hand around her waist and tug her closer. She's tucked against me, able to feel my beating heart through my chest and my cock pulsing against her belly.

"Orc!"

We break the kiss so fast I wonder if one of my tusks might have sliced her cheek as we both look toward the noise. Five humans. They don't look like adults, but I've recently proven I can't determine humans' ages.

One thing is certain, they're looking for a fight. Two carry bats, I can smell at least one gun, though I don't see it.

"What are you doing to this human, Otherfucker?"

"Run home," I urge her. How is it I never asked her name, or where she lived? Still, I order, "Run!"

I can take them, all of them. Although the gun is a wild card.

"Come with me." She's pulling my arm.

I want to argue, to tell her I can fight them, but there's no time for talk. Her tight lips and narrowed eyes tell me she's not going to leave without me, so I follow her through the maze of playground equipment and into the night.

She seems to know this place like the back of her hand, darting into the black night even though I know her night vision is poor compared to mine. We run through an alleyway, then a vacant lot, then zigzag between low-slung apartments until we arrive at her building.

The exterior of the building doesn't inspire much confidence. It's a dilapidated structure, with peeling and cracked paint, revealing layers of neglect.

My senses are on high alert as adrenaline courses through me. I can hear her fumbling with her keys as I stand with my back to her, ready to take all comers. Her hands tremble as she unlocks the heavy metal door. We hurry inside and slam it shut behind us, making sure the lock engages before she leads me toward the stairs.

The dim hallway is just as grim as the exterior. Flickering fluorescent lights barely illuminate the stained walls, giving the place a gloomy atmosphere. The air is heavy with the scent of decay and neglect. Despite how I've seen humans live on TV, this place looks as though it belongs in the Zone.

She leads me up a flight of stairs, the worn-out carpeting muffling our footsteps. There's a lot of noise, considering the time of night. The faint sound of music, TV, and muffled voices drift through the hallways. It's a cacophony that adds to my growing unease. This place doesn't feel safe, especially with those humans hot on our heels.

When we reach her apartment door, this time there is no fumbling as she quickly unlocks it, ushering me inside. The moment I step in, my senses are assaulted by something entirely unexpected. A sense of sanctuary. It's a stark contrast to the outside world, where danger lurks around every corner.

The cozy living room's lights cast a gentle glow, illuminating the room. Every wall is adorned with colorful artwork except for the space filled with bookshelves overflowing with books. This place is a refuge.

As I take in the surroundings, I notice the subtle details that make her apartment uniquely hers. A plush red couch sits against one wall, accompanied by a cozy armchair covered in a patchwork quilt.

Her personal touches are everywhere. A collection of succulents lines the windowsill. A record player sits on a nearby shelf near a stack of vinyl records waiting to be played.

But it's the single framed photograph center stage on the bookshelf that catches my attention. It captures a whimsical moment at a carnival, her laughter frozen in time. It's a reminder that beyond her struggles, she's still capable of finding joy.

As I absorb the peacefulness of her small space, I'm struck by a need to protect not just her, but her sanctuary. The urgent desire to keep her safe and shield her from any harm surges through me, making my heart race.

But the voices of those humans still echo in my mind, a reminder of the danger looming outside these walls. We may be momentarily safe here, but the urgent need for a plan weighs heavily on me.

"I go to that park all the time. That's never happened before." Her voice is tight, her breathing still accelerated.

I shrug, not wanting to say what I'm thinking—that I've already brought her bad luck.

"I could have fought them. You should have run while I kept them at bay." I don't mention the gun. That might terrify her.

"Yep. You could have fought them. Looking at you..." She looks me up and down, which reignites the connection sparking between us, "Looking at you, you probably would have won. Unless one of them had a knife, or a gun, or a cellphone. One call to the police and the word of five humans against one Other and you would have wound up being the bad guy. The night would have ended with you in jail. Or worse."

"What if I *am* the bad guy? What if the dumbest thing you've ever done is to invite me into your home?"

Buy on Amazon.com/FREE in KU or get the audiobook for only $5.99 on my Alanaverse store: shopalanakhan.com

MANY THANKS

Thanks to you, dear reader. Let's face it, it would be hard to keep writing without knowing people enjoy my books! I love hearing from you! alanakhanauthor@gmail.com

Thanks to my super early readers who give feedback about plot and characters. Special thanks to Dr. Lee, my Development Editor and Stephanie, my PA from across the pond, and Naomi S. who has an eye for adding extras and upping my game.

Also thanks to my beta team. They manage to tell me what doesn't work for them and catch any errors that have slipped through. Thanks to: Nancy R., Holly S., Hilga H., Jhane M., Anne H., Michelle B, Kelly B., and Marianne K.

About Alana Khan

Alana Khan is a Pinnacle Award-winning, USA TODAY Bestselling author whose pen traverses galaxies and explores the extraordinary.

In a life as diverse as her stories, Alana boasts IMDB film credits, thrilling Harley adventures on open roads, and a stint as a professional spoon player—because, why not?

With a background as a psychotherapist, she delves into the human psyche, enriching her storytelling.

Join her on fantastical journeys through her novels, where cosmic romance and monstrous love merge with spice as hot as a Carolina Reaper chili pepper.

Want to read the next books in the series? Help yourself to 15% off anything in the store including dozens of $5.99 audios.

Go to my website for FREE books at www.alanakhan.com

WANT MORE OF MY BOOKS?

Galaxy Gladiators Alien Abduction Romance Series

This 19-book series can be read as standalones, although it's fun to read them in order because the books are full of that rich, delicious found-family trope where people with nothing in common form connections that are stronger than blood. You'll grow to love this ragtag bunch of escaped slaves and the human women they rescue. Or do the women rescue them? Full of action, romance, and spice.

Galaxy Pirates Alien Abduction Romance Series

As the name implies, these alien Robin Hoods are scoundrels and rascals. Opportunists all, they've never met a human damsel in distress who wasn't worth saving. Full of action, romance, daring capers, and spice. P.S. The bad guys always lose their money and our pirates walk away all the richer.

Galaxy Sanctuary Alien Abduction Romance Series

There's one thing about flying across the galaxy righting wrongs (the Gladiator series) or stealing from people who deserve it (the Pirates series)--you can't have kids on a fighting ship. Some worthy freed gladiators end up on planet Fairea and find themselves on a safe parcel of acreage, yet in desperate need of funds. Between jostling for control of the operation and the lengths they must go to stay safe and keep the lights on, there is plenty of action, romance, and steam.

Galaxy Warriors Alien Abduction Romance Series

What was I thinking writing 19 books in the Galaxy Gladiators series? Call it temporary insanity. This series is similar to Gladiators, but lets new readers jump in without knowing any backstory. Action, adventure, my trademark spice, and romance.

Galaxy Games Hostile Planet Alien Romance Series

All the heart-pounding passion and gut-clenching action I could cram onto the page. This series will grab you by the throat from the first page and never let you go. More action and hotter than previous series. And love. Did I forget to mention love?

Rescued by the Monsters Reverse Harem Romance series

In a future dystopian Earth, males have been spliced with animal DNA. Human women have been reduced to chattel and when they say no, even once, they're banished Down Below to where the "monsters" live. This series will soon have you wondering just who the monsters are as the human women each bond with three adoring human/animal hybrids.

Arixxia Fields: A Steamy Small-Town Alien Romance Series

Are you ready to party? I imagine so, after reading all the drama in all my previous series. Each of these books is short, sexy, romantic, and FUN. Each revolves around a holiday. Check them out.

Hybrid Hearts Series

Bred to be soldiers, these rescued genetically engineered males are all given a new lease on life. How does the United States military plan to do that? They create an isolated town with cute shops and train the males in new jobs. How about a sexy lion-man baker for starters?

Galaxy Artificials Series

Packed with passion and spice, USA TODAY Bestselling author Alana Khan brings robots to life in this science fiction romance series. Oh yeah, she manages to give the metallic buckets of bolts smokin' hot humanoid bodies, too.

Orcfire Series (written with Aria Vale)

Twenty-five years ago, thousands of Others (orcs, nagas, minotaurs, and other species only known in fairytales) fell onto the burning sands of the Mojave Desert with no way to go home. They were rounded up by the U.S. Military and placed in a fenced enclosure on the outskirts of Los Angeles. The OrcFire series features one hot, green, tusked orc as the hero of each book as they battle fires and so much more to find their happily ever after. The OrcFire series will be hot, hot, hot in all ways.

Cosmic Kissed (Earthbound Alien Romance Series)

This fun duet manages to make reptilians sexy (trust me). Two alien brothers are abducted to Earth. Each gets his own book and manages to get the girl in this upside-down take on alien abduction.

Monster on Board (written with USA TODAY Bestselling author Ava Ross)

What happens when two USA TODAY Bestselling sci-fi romance authors get together to have some fun? We write these entertaining, short, and sexy books set in space. They're all standalones, so take your pick of an orc, an ogre, a merman, or a hunky blue-winged alien. Or take them all!

Treasured by the Zinn Alien Abduction Romance Series

The US government gave the Zinns permission to take human women as wives. Let's just say the unsuspecting women, who know nothing of this unsavory deal, are none too happy—until they fall in love.

Mastered by the Zinn Alien Abduction Romance Series

Welcome to the enticing universe of 'Mastered by the Zinn,' a secret arrangement that's endured for centuries.

The government's shadowy pact with the alien Zinn species allows for the abduction of human women in exchange for cutting-edge military technology. It's a clandestine game of risk and reward, desire and dominance.

Billionaire Doms of Blackstone (written as Deja Blue)

Alana's only contemporaries. The heroes are all doms, the women are only happy to serve.

Box Sets

Galaxy Gladiators Alien Abduction Romance Series Books 1 to 10 plus bonus

Galaxy Gladiators Alien Abduction Romance Series Books 11 to 19

Galaxy Pirates Alien Abduction Romance Series

Galaxy Sanctuary Alien Abduction Romance Series

Galaxy Games Hostile Planet Alien Romance Series

Galaxy Warriors Alien Abduction Romance Series

Arixxia Fields Series

Rescued by the Monsters Series

First In Series : Zar / Sextus / Arzz

First In Series : Zar / Sextus / Arzz / Thran

Treasured by the Zinn Alien Abduction Romance Series

Mastered by the Zinn Alien Abduction Romance Series

Cosmic Kissed Duo Box Set